AF225512

THE FARNSWORTH FILES

A Family's Tragic Past Discovered by Chance

WILLIAM H. CHRIST, JR.

ISBN: 978-1-63795-415-7   (Paperback Edition)
ISBN: 978-1-63795-416-4   (Hardcover Edition)
ISBN: 978-1-63795-409-6   (E-book Edition)

Book Ordering Information

Phone Number: 315 288-7939 ext. 1000 or 347-901-4920
Email: info@globalsummithouse.com
Global Summit House
www.globalsummithouse.com

Printed in the United States of America

This Book is dedicated to
my Best Friend and long-time Associate,
& Vietnam Era Veteran
Archbishop Joseph F. Steward, D.D.

Prologue

U.S. Military Prison, Fort Leavenworth, Kansas
1984

An infamous medical physician was paid a visit today by a former Farnsworth College antiwar radical student. The visitor was a graduate from the class of 1973. He notified his incarcerated friend about a shift in the college's attitude regarding its past former security issues. The college's current academic dean was experiencing serious health issues with cancer, along with some reoccurring psychological problems. The past ten years, without the inmate's special "handling," have made many things on campus very difficult.

Together with this inmate's connections and influence, the visitor had recently earned his doctorate. The visitor informed him that within a short time from now, he would become Farnsworth's new academic dean.

As the newly elected dean, the visitor emphasized his interest about becoming another puppet for the influential inmate while he served out the remainder of his sentence. During the meeting, the inmate indicated how he would be very pleased to assist the new dean. Through correspondence, he will advise the dean how to maintain total control of the subversive activities at Farnsworth College. As dean, he would soon be able to reintroduce many of the mind-controlling security programs, which the inmate had instituted nearly fifteen years earlier. The new dean, Joey, had previously married his former college hippie girlfriend,

Kiki, in 1980. Kiki and Joey had "volunteered" for the notorious inmate's top secret medical research program. Those experiments were conducted at Fort Douglas, located near Farnsworth College, beginning back in 1969. She and her husband had willingly participated in and supported the newly developed test trails through 1974. That is when Joey's friend had been arrested by the U.S. Army for misusing military medical funding, and was sentenced to twenty years in Leavenworth Prison.

Ten years later
Fort Leavenworth, Kansas
August 1994

The former military doctor was escorted by military police to the entrance of the prison. He had been given a dishonorable discharge, civilian clothes, an ID, and a travel voucher. Once the gates closed behind him, he was again a free man.

The twenty years behind bars had taken a physical toll but did nothing to resolve the doctor's determination to gain access to his inheritance. Many men and women had suffered greatly between 1969 and 1974 under this cruel doctor's calculated decisions. He had become obsessed with greed over his partners' success during those turbulent antiwar demonstrating years. Money was pouring into a secret account from several sources.

Skillfully, only after nearly each major player's part ended under mysterious circumstances, was the doctor able to tap in and control the money flow. His access, though, lasted for a little more than a year. He was then betrayed by one of his newer players. The doctor's intricate plan was then totally exposed.

He was captured, tried, and sentenced to twenty years in the military prison at Leavenworth.

Prior to his conviction in August 1974, army Colonel Travis Cummings, MD, operated a million-dollar drug ring. Following a major setback, in June 1972, he acquired a small abandoned factory in the city of Silopanna. It was near the Metro D.C. area. By the fall of that year, his mind-controlled security guards protected it. While still connected with the army, he secretly resumed producing large quantities of the newly modified psychotic drug, Sernyl. The formula had been patented by Farnsworth College's chemistry professor, Henry Prestol. The patent was surrendered, through blackmail, to Dr. Cummings.

Now released from prison, civilian, former doctor Cummings quietly returned to his Silopanna facility in Maryland. Within twenty-four hours of his release, Dr. Cummings had acquired many fake documents, including a military promotion. Since he was a convicted felon and unable to practice medicine, he was at least able to set up his private research lab and resume "reconditioning" some new student and adult volunteers. His former colleague, Dr. Joseph "Joey" Henson, PhD, helped. Joseph, the current dean at Farnsworth College, was very eager to assist the "good" doctor.

Dean Henson additionally introduced Dr. Cummings to his administrative assistant, Stephan Vognar, and political science professor, Roger Hill. Henson knew that both Stephan and Roger had been hooked on prescription drugs for years. They were each very willing to become Cumming's henchmen.

Those two, along with several others, soon were reconditioned and began distributing his drugs to an entire new generation on Farnsworth and other nearby college campuses. Money, once again, began to be collected and used for further "research and development."

The doctor also searched out and found Farnsworth's former psychology professor, Dr. William Gray, PhD, living in Georgetown. Bill was operating a private practice as a therapist.

After Dr. Cummings contacted Bill Gray, the psychologist became very suspicious. The doctor expressed sincere regret over his past harsh treatment from then Farnsworth's dean, Trisha Alexander, in 1972. Cummings also expressed that he would be pleased to be considered his friend once again.

Tuesday, September 13, 1994

Dr. Cummings and several of his henchmen drove up and parked near the main entrance to the Pennsylvania State Penitentiary outside Pittsburg. They had come to escort another former inmate and Farnsworth College student, Teddy Lancer, back home. Cummings knew for some time about his pending release date. He also realized Teddy could pose a threat to his new mission about the missing fortune. Teddy had just completed serving his twenty-two years for an arson fire bombing in Ambersburg back in 1972. Teddy, along with Joey Henson and Ricky Sheridan, Jr., were then Colonel Cummings premier campus student radicals at Farnsworth College.

Dr. Cummings and his men now waited inside his stretched limo with its black windows. Soon, a yellow taxi drove up and parked near the prison's entrance. Cummings had one of his men quickly approach and pay off the driver. The taxi then sped off.

Within a short time, a weary-looking, forty-two-year-old gray-haired individual emerged wearing a wrinkled brown suit and carrying a bag containing his personal effects.

"I was expecting a cab, not a stretched limo!" exclaimed the newly freed man.

As one of Cumming's men opened limo door, Dr. Cummings said, "Welcome back, Teddy. It's been a long time."

"Well, hello, Doctor! Aren't you a sight for sore eyes?"

"Hello, Teddy. You're looking well."

"I'm really surprised and glad you were able to come by and pick me up."

After exchanging handshakes, Teddy entered the limo and they drove away. Following a brief exchange regarding his interest in also finding the missing fortune, Teddy was quickly injected with a hypodermic needle and rendered unconscious.

There's got to be a way to rid me of these characters who want shares of my missing fortune, the doctor thought to himself.

By evening, the limo had arrived at Dr. Cummings's warehouse in Silopanna. His men placed Teddy unconscious onto a hospital gurney.

He was then wheeled into the rear of the warehouse containing one of the secret drug labs. Once there, preparations were begun for some after-midnight mind conditioning. •

1

Farnsworth Liberal Arts College
Clementsburg, Maryland
September 14, 1994
Day One: Wednesday Morning

Farnsworth College had just begun the fall semester of 1994. The campus was filled with youthful students anxious to start or continue their higher education. The sports complex was ready for their first home basketball and football openers. Workers inside the newly constructed library were still installing the latest computer technology. Each department on campus appeared fully staffed and eager to welcome another academic year.

Behind the serene campus settings, there was an air of apprehension among certain faculty members, including the academic dean, Dr. Joseph Henson, PhD. This September represented a special month on a lot of individuals' calendars. It marked an anniversary that many people on campus would like to completely forget. Yet for some, it was the moment they had waited far too long a time for. It certainly was an odd sort of homecoming that could now happen at any time.

Fog still covered the Farnsworth College campus parking lot around 8:15 a.m. as two twenty-two-year-old Farnsworth students, Kyle Sheridan and Jennifer Howser, pulled into a parking space in his yellow Mustang. The usual fifteen-minute drive from southern

Pennsylvania had taken nearly an hour. Both postgraduates agreed that this nine-o'clock graduate class in architecture was important for their master's degree, but for some reason, today it really took some serious convincing.

They soon were joined this morning by other sleepy-eyed students as they quickly crossed in front of the new library. The group passed the college's chapel bell tower as it was tolling. The sun was trying unsuccessfully to pierce the fog as Kyle entered the political science building and Jennifer proceeded to the student union for their coffees.

He told Jennifer, "I'll see if Professor Hill needs anything done before his morning classes begin."

"Fine, I'll meet you at McNeil Hall in fifteen minutes with our coffee."

His noninterest in what was going on behind the scenes at Farnsworth College gave Kyle the opportunity to get his graduate assistant position.

Kyle did feel somewhat uncomfortable when he quietly entered the office and inadvertently overheard a telephone conversation between Professor Roger Hill and the academic dean, Joseph Henson's, assistant, Stephan Vognar. What began as a quiet and normal call soon erupted into a shouting match. The professor, facing away from his desk, did not notice Kyle entering.

"Please, Vognar! I need some of the doctor's 'special' shit now!"

The dean's administrative assistant responded, "Shut up, Professor, you fucking bastard! Listen to me! You can't get it now. Our supply of Sernyl has run out, and the good doctor needs a payment or a personnel exchange first. Then we'll both be able to get our new shipment."

The professor, now in a perspiring state of agitation, yelled, "Damn it, Vognar! Please talk to Dr. Cummings or anyone else in charge. They'll help us!"

"How do I know who's in charge? Those bastards have begun to rotate their staff and keep us vulnerable. Oh, hold on, Dean Henson needs something. I've got to go. Call him yourself. Goodbye, you sorry son of a bitch, and don't call me again. You understand"

"No! Please . . . Please help me!"

"Not today, Professor. Use your own damn resources."

"Very well, I will. And then let's see who begs!"

Professor Hill slammed down the telephone receiver. He was a man who resembled a leftover fifty-year-old hippie with long hair in a ponytail, graying beard, and narrow wire-rimmed bifocals. Upon seeing Kyle, wide-eyed and mouth open, standing next to the closed door, it startled him. The professor begged his pardon and pleaded to Kyle, "Mr. Sheridan, please don't repeat anything you just overheard."

"Sure, Professor Hill, I never talk about other people's business to anyone."

"Mr. Sheridan, listen to me. Here are some words of advice. There are certain individuals currently on campus who want to see new changes made. Many of us don't."

"This campus seems fine to me, Professor. Of course I'm kind of new here. My undergraduate work was done at the state college."

"I understand, and that's how it needs to stay."

"Professor Hill, I'm finished grading your tests, and I have your things laid out for today's classes."

"Fine, Mr. Sheridan, just one thing before you leave."

"Sure, what's that?"

"Professor Moore needs these slides for her class tomorrow in the lecture hall. Could you drop them off after your classes today?"

"No problem. My class there is after lunch. Good day, Professor. Are you sure you're okay?"

"I'm fine. It's just a slight migraine. I'll survive, good at that, you know."

As soon as Kyle left his office and closed the door, Professor Hill grabbed the phone and made another call to the information operator to help him locate another number. Once the operator had found it, he made note of it. He excitedly dialed the number from his desk phone.

"Doctor's Office, how may I direct your call?"

"Hello. This is political science professor Roger Hill at Farnsworth College. Could you kindly put me through to Dr. Travis Cummings, MD? I have a lead he may be very interested in and probably would like to follow up on."

"Of course, Professor Hill, the doctor will be with you shortly."

Once Dr. Cummings had greeted Professor Hill on the phone, the professor stated, "Sir! I really need some of your special drugs."

"I can, only if you are able to meet my specific requirements."

"I realize that, Doctor. How does my new graduate assistant sound like? His name is Kyle Sheridan, son of JP Sheridan."

"Good God above!" exclaimed Dr. Cummings, shouting into the phone receiver. "After twenty fucking years of languishing in the depths of hell, this is the best news anyone could have possibly given me today."

"May he assist you on your quest?" asked Professor Hill.

"I have prayed and planned for this day for a long, long time, Professor. And you will be rewarded for helping me reclaim what is justifiably mine."

"I'll be glad to help in any way I can for some of your latest formula drugs."

Dr. Cummings asked the professor to physically describe Kyle. "He's about six foot, has a muscular build, jet-black hair, and chilled features."

"Sounds just like his father," replied the doctor.

Following that, Professor Hill remarked, "Your work on this campus, over twenty years ago, was truly groundbreaking. You continually remain highly regarded as a true innovator. What you began back then was so brilliant that it has endured throughout this entire next generation."

"Thank you, Professor. It will be a pleasure bringing you onboard with young Mr. Sheridan."

The two men then exchanged some additional information and set up a time and place to meet and discuss the doctor's new plan in detail. Professor Hill hung up his phone as the hall bell began ringing, indicating the change of class. Feeling relieved and a bit calmer, he left for class quickly, grabbing his briefcase and closing his office door behind him.

Dr. Travis Cummings, MD, hung up his phone call from Professor Hill smiling. He had just been told the good news that JP Sheridan, one of his participants in his former medical research, had a son, Kyle, who was now working with Professor Roger Hill as his graduate assistant. Dr. Cummings sensed a feeling of confidence. He again had a new key ingredient to help him locate and perhaps lead him to his lost fortune. He must now figure out a game plan. Soon thereafter, he placed another call to Farnsworth College's Administration Offices.

"Farnsworth College, how may I direct your call?" replied the operator.

"Dean Henson's assistant, Stephan Vognar, please." Shortly, Stephan answered, and he said, "This is Dr. Travis Cummings. Please listen carefully to what I have to say. Do not identify me to anyone, and you will be properly taken care of."

Stephan responded, almost in a whisper, "Of course, anything I can do to help is an honor, sir!"

"I have a mission for you. Lister up, soldier! Downstairs in the basement of your building is a storage room marked A-2. Inside that room is an old locked wooden file cabinet labeled 'Property of U.S. Army.' I need that cabinet moved tonight over to the political science building. Put a cover over it and place the file cabinet into the storage room that adjoins Professor Hill's office."

"I understand, sir! That can easily be arranged."

"Good! Now, there are just a few more things. First, make sure no one sees you moving the cabinet. Do it after hours. Secondly, once it's in the room, conceal it with boxes. Make it appear that it's always been there."

The doctor then asked Stephan, "Lastly, drop over to my lab today and pick up the file cabinet's key and something special."

Within an hour, the doctor was notified of a guest at the front entrance. Once he entered the lobby, the doctor welcomed Dean Henson's administrative assistant, Stephan Vognar.

"Hello, Dr. Cummings. There certainly seems to be a real problem with political science professor Roger Hill."

"How's that, Stephan?"

"Whatever he's on is really making him psychotic. You know, severe mood swings."

"I just talked to Hill about an hour ago. He told me about his new graduate assistant, Kyle Sheridan. That lad's going to assist me in my quest!"

"How so, Doctor? Who is he?"

"He's the son of the infamous Master Sergeant JP Sheridan."

"Huh. I never heard of him."

"Back in the early 1970s, JP brought in tons of money selling my formula for Sernyl. Farnsworth's then chemistry professor, Henry Prestol, and I created a new formula to better control mood swings.

JP Sheridan was a real success story with our modified version of the Peace Pill."

"Oh, now I understand. That was like ancient history."

"Yeah, Stephan," he said, patting him on the back. "I guess to you it might seem that way," said the doctor with a smile.

"But, sir, Professor Hill has told me that he has really become a heavy user. He's combining several different drugs and is demanding I help him hook him up today."

"Well, let's see. Our production is a mere fraction of what we used to make in the early 1970s. Probably, within the next seventy-two hours, we'll have what everyone needs."

"I hope so. He's become a real pain in my ass."

"I completely understand. Addicts tend to be that way. Oh yes, and there's some other things you'll need." He handed Stephan a hypodermic syringe and the old file cabinet's key, saying, "Be certain that Professor Hill is conditioned to instruct the Sheridan boy about locating the filing cabinet."

"Certainly, Dr. Cummings, I completely understand."

"Thank you in advance, Stephan, for helping to bring that damn file cabinet over to Hill's office later after dark. Oh yes, here's something for you too."

Dr. Cummings then gave Stephan a prescription bottle containing several pills.

"It's a real honor to serve you, sir, and welcome back!" replied Stephan with a smart military-style salute.

2

Farnsworth College
September 15, 1994
Day Two: Thursday

By ten o'clock, this morning's fog had dissipated and a new bright, cool September day had emerged. Trees in the higher elevations of Maryland's Catoctin Mountains still remained mostly summer green. Within the next several weeks, those same trees would begin to turn spectacular autumn colors. Farnsworth College's proud tradition was being extended into another new semester. Across the campus at the Field House, preparations were well underway for the season's basketball and football games.

From an upper-level window in the administration building, the current dean, Dr. Joseph Henson, PhD, a former Farnsworth student and a graduate with the class of 1972, surveyed the peaceful campus quad. It had not always been so. There were the memories from his early college years. There were still employed staffers who today know what had really happened . . . but were sworn to secrecy for their own job security. Now, here is another new class of freshmen who could ask an innocent question and find themselves expelled and headed back home or worse. They too could experience what had happened to dozens and dozens of other students before them if they dared to be overly curious.

Focusing on the approaching figures of Kyle and Jennifer crossing the street, the dean could see a familiar resemblance . . . but no, "Surely they're all gone by now," he mumbled as he closed his eyes. Within an instant, he was transported back in a daydream flash to the campus of twenty-four years earlier.

Farnsworth Liberal Arts College Quad
May 1970

Peace signs hung in the nearby dogwood trees. Banners were everywhere, demanding our exit from Vietnam and stopping the draft. Students milling around with long hair, beards, beads, and tie-dyed clothes paraded about in the quad. Teddy Lancer, Joey Henson, Ricky Sheridan, Jr., Melanie Dulane, and Kiki Flaund were among those people. They and hundreds of others were searching for knowledge that their parents were unable to provide. Farnsworth College had all the answers, problems, and questions that these Flower Children generation needed. It was the beginning of the 1970s.

The student protesters were extremely vocal, and their anger was aimed back at that very same administration building's third-floor corner office and seeing a glimpse of the college's first female dean, a Ms. Tricia Alexander. She stood there watching out and looking down at the demonstrating students who were leading the parade. They were all voicing their sentiments in another huge anti-Vietnam War student demonstration around the campus quad.

Dean Henson awoke from his recollecting daydream and spoke out loud to himself, "We survived. Farnsworth College survived. Dean Alexander and her blood money did not," while continuing to look out of the third-story corner window.

"Excuse me, Dean," stated his secretary over the intercom.

"There's a visitor here to see you and says he's an alumnus. He said it's very urgent."

Returning to matters at hand, the dean said, "Very well, Stephan. Send in our guest."

Entering the oak-paneled office, the stranger, wearing black leather gloves, a tan trench coat, and velour hat, moved toward the desk, saying, "Good morning, Dean Henson. You remember me?"

"Oh my god! Teddy Lancer! What in heaven's name are you doing here?" said the dean as he stood to warmly greet his visitor with an extended hand.

The visitor did not engage the handshake. "It's been a long fucking time, Joey!"

Acting with an appearance of innocence, the dean said, "I didn't know about your release from the state prison."

"Yea, you should've been there. Dr. Cummings was."

"It was all a big mistake. I swear it!"

"Joey, I never forgot that night of the firebombing."

"Why, in God's name, have you come back here now?"

With his familiar wide grin, he said, "I've brought you something special just for the occasion, you old son of a bitch."

"Really?" replied the dean, adjusting his glasses.

Suddenly a ten-inch knife emerged from under the trench coat and, in an instant, was plunged deep into the dean's chest by the intruder.

"Oh god!" murmured the dean as he slumped forward onto his desktop. Dean Henson's body quickly became limp.

The deadly visitor silently moved quietly to the corner window and raised the sash. He pulled himself up over an ancient radiator and climbed onto the window's ledge. He then reached for the wrought iron handrail of the old metal fire escape. Looking about, he saw the broad expanse of the modern-day campus. Thirty-five feet below was freedom. Holding on carefully, he descended the first ladder.

Upon reaching the platform, the ladder felt somewhat shaky against the 150-year-old stone building. Then it happened. A rusted bolt slid free of the crumbing mortar, then another. The man in the trench coat looked in horror as the platform separated from the building and began to fall. Screaming and tumbling downward, the murderer himself was crushed by the immense weight of the falling metal fire escape.

"Did you see that?" yelled Kyle to Jennifer along with some fellow students. "Come on! That guy must be hurt pretty bad."

As many students ran toward the building, they heard shouting coming from the open third-story window. Looking up, they saw Stephan Vognar yelling, "The dean has just been murdered!"

"My god! How awful a thing to happen this morning!" cried Jennifer to her fiancé.

"Any of you know this dude?" asked one of the students first on the scene. Those about shook their heads negatively.

Within minutes, campus police notified the paramedics from the nearby Clementsburg Volunteer Fire and Rescue Department about the death of Dean Henson. Shortly thereafter, they arrived with sirens blaring. Soon, members of the local press joined the area medical examiner at the chaotic scene. During the commotion, statements and crime scene photos were taken.

"Reminiscent of twenty some years ago, I guess," stated an elderly gray-haired civilian spectator standing nearby Kyle and Jennifer.

"Who are you, sir, if you don't mind?"

"I'm Dr. Travis Cummings, MD, U.S. Army, retired."

"Hello, Dr. Cummings, I'm Professor Roger Hill's graduate assistant, Kyle Sheridan, and this is my fiancée, Ms. Jennifer Howser."

"It's a pleasure to meet both of you."

"Dr. Cummings, do you mean to say others died here at Farnsworth College?" asked a wide-eyed Jennifer.

"They really never did find out how their first female dean and her supposedly lover, Professor Prestol, vanished mysteriously."

"Are you referring to Ms. Trisha Alexander?" inquired Kyle.

"Some say she was involved with the drugs, and the hippies did her and her lover in, along with many other students and facility members."

Kyle, standing with his arms crossed and a serious frown, said, "I never heard of that!"

"And the others?" asked an inquiring and anxious Jennifer.

"Army intelligence knows what happened here at Farnsworth during the late sixties and early seventies. But the truth is probably locked away forever in some damn underground vault at Fort Douglas."

"Interesting, thanks for the history lesson. I'll put it in my research notes for class next Monday."

"Do that," the older but very physically in-shape medical doctor said with a smile.

3

Kyle reflected for a moment on his current situation and commented to Dr. Cummings, "I wish I knew more about those years."

"How's that, Mr. Sheridan?"

"It seems that my parents and my girlfriend's parents each attended this college in the early 1970s. Ever since Jen and I met, she's talked a lot about how she longs to find out about her own parents' college years. I suppose I'm curious about mine too."

"What are your parents' names?"

"My daddy was a highly decorated Vietnam army veteran named John Paul Sheridan. His family and friends just called him JP."

"Hmmm. Does not ring a bell, sorry," he said with a frown while acting very nonchalant.

"That's all right. He was quite a gifted artist when he was young and had a passion for finding and collecting Civil War artifacts.

Growing up, he used to live in Gettysburg, Pennsylvania. My mom's a former model from Washington, D.C.," Kyle then added. "My daddy's brother, my uncle, Ricky Sheridan, Jr., also attended here. It's ironic though. I'm driving his 1969 Mustang again on this same campus today."

"I'm sure they're all very proud of what you are doing now."

"Yeah, I suppose so. Thanks, Dr. Cummings."

Kyle and Jennifer left the chaotic scene, leaving the double murders to the professionals and were about to go to class when a loud speaker system notified the student body, "Due to the tragic and sudden death today of our beloved Dean Henson, all of today's afternoon classes have been canceled. A memorial service will be held this coming Sunday afternoon at 2:00 p.m. in the college chapel. Students and faculty members are all invited to attend."

Gettysburg, Pennsylvania
Spring 1969

John Paul Sheridan's legacy began as an awkward, lanky seventeen-year-old Gettysburg High School junior. JP was basically an underachiever. He was an average nonathletic student with a passion for art, collecting things, and loving nature and wild animals.

JP was constantly overshadowed by his able-to-do-nothing-wrong year-older brother, Richard, Jr. Ricky was now a senior at Gettysburg High School.

Following his graduation, he would become a freshman at Farnsworth College in the class of 1972 on an athletic scholarship. The nearby college was located just south of the Mason Dixon Line in the central highlands of Maryland.

JP and his jock brother, Ricky, Jr., lived together with their parents, Richard, Sr., and Mary Sheridan, in a two-story brick townhouse. The rear one-story section of the house was build prior to the Civil War. The two-story brick was added during the 1880s with a round attic turret, which was a popular Queen Anne's period architectural feature. The Gettysburg Civil War battlefield surrounded the town. J. P explored the scene of this great American conflict on many occasions with sketch pad in hand. His artistic talent remained unquestioned by his parents and teachers alike.

His brother, Ricky, with his acid comments and biting critiques, gave JP even more reason to shine. He also was fortunate to have collected several items from the nearby battlefield. These items where proudly displayed in his bedroom's trophy case unlike his brother's trophy case, which was filled with sports achievements.

The boys' father, Richard, Sr., operated a local construction company and was also actively involved with other business owners working on downtown improvements. His wife, Mary, was an English literature teacher at the senior high school. The Gettysburg Community Association had recently awarded both of the Sheridan parents for their outstanding community achievements.

Richard, Sr. was high-spirited, energetic, and usually able to consume vast quantities of alcohol with his friends and associates. Mary, trying to lead a reasonable Christian household, frowned on her husband's drinking. He never abused her in front of their sons, but the boys suspected things weren't quite right between their parents.

Ricky maintained the only source of his pop's pride. The boy was nearly elevated to sainthood by his pop when he helped the Sharpsburg High's basketball team win the state's championship title. Ricky did a free throw from midcourt at the buzzer. That feat clinched his athletic scholarship to Farnsworth College.

JP realized early on that he was a disappointment to his dad because he was not a jock. His mom often came to the boy's defense before his intoxicated father could pull his belt free of his pants. JP once, though, when his mother was not around, was discovered with an unauthorized use of a simple paint paddle from his pop's toolbox. He needed the paddle to mix some paint for an art project in junior high and had forgotten to ask Pop's permission. The paddle eventually broke from the many times it was used during his drunken father's rage on his little bare ass.

The time came last month for JP to find a date for the upcoming junior prom. He shyly asked a very attractive classmate, Suzanne Hardesty, to be his date. At first, she seemed surprised since she had not looked at him seriously.

He was excited when she replied with acceptance.

Following that, he asked her to keep it a secret. "Please don't let my brother find out that you're my prom date. He'll hurt me if he finds out. He never approves of any of my decisions nor my friends."

She assured him she would keep their prom date a secret. JP felt relieved since the junior and senior proms were being held on the same night. He felt empowered that he could now brag to his brother that she was to be his date.

"Prom night is coming up soon. Who's your date, son?" asked his mom at the dinner table that night with both his pop and brother Ricky present.

"I don't quite know just yet," he responded.

"Don't worry, Mom. He's too shy to ask any really hot girl," said Ricky. And, turning to JP, added, "Loser!"

"I'm not a loser!"

"That's right, JP. Take your time. There are plenty of attractive young ladies to choose from in your class, son," his mother assured him.

"Homely chicks!" was his brother's side comment.

"I like several of the girls." Trying to quickly change the direction of the conversation, he asked Ricky, "So who's your senior prom's date?"

"Melanie Dulane will naturally be with me that night," he said a big grin.

"Great choice, son," commented his pop with approval.

"Oh! Her," said JP. "She's in my pants. Oh! I mean my class!"

"That's right, little bro. I know you been dating her all year! I even asked her if you all were doing the nasty about month ago, and she said you were!" he boasted.

"You little snooping bastard!" cried Ricky.

"Mom! Tell this jerk I'm not a bastard please."

"Boys! Boys! Calm down, and no, JP, you are not."

"Ricky can have anyone he wants, including the beautiful Melanie," his pop said proudly.

JP left the table feeling totally frustrated once more. Ricky had won again.

He ran upstairs to his room and called Suzanne on his extension phone.

"Hello, Suzanne. JP here"

"Why are you calling me tonight?"

"My brother just called me a bastard at the dinner table over him and Melanie having sex together."

"Oh my! He had asked me to do it with him too a while back."

"Did you?"

"I, I kind of guess so. It was such an honor and a thrill to be in bed with our school's star athlete. Sorry, I forgot to mention it to you, JP, bye."

He threw down the phone receiver and fell on the bed sobbing. He felt really betrayed.

Kyle Sheridan, son of JP Sheridan, believed that his decision not to get involved with Farnsworth's internal operations or campus staff personalities seemed right for now. What did he care if the professors and administrators knew each other or slept with each other's husband or spouse or even if they did drugs? Why would it matter to him if a lowly freshman recently was expelled for cheating on a test, or a college jock tested positive for drugs and got kicked off of the team last week? These things occur often on all college campuses, and he never let it bother him.

4

Day Three:
Friday, September 16, 1994

The gray morning soon gave way to the overly bright fluorescent-lighted corridors of McNeil Hall's engineering wing. After commenting about the glare, Kyle shielded his eyes for a moment and then repositioned his baseball cap over his black hair.

Jennifer politely took his hand and gave it a reassuring squeeze. Her bright smile and long blond hair made her a true campus beauty.

"Here, finish your fifty-cent coffee. You'll need it to stay awake during the class."

Shortly, the lower-level classroom was filled with youthful students as the short and very preppie-looking red-headed Irish Professor Elizabeth Moore entered. She was in her late thirties and had already been divorced twice. She was a true feminist of the 1990s. She was a tenured facility and had been appointed by the late Dean Henson in 1985.

Kyle handed the professor her slides as she entered.

"Good morning, class. Before we begin, I would appreciate if you'd stand for a moment of silence in honor of our late dean, Dr. Joseph Henson."

Following that, the students took their seats, and she began by saying, "Today's lecture is about the development of Georgian architecture and the influence of neoclassical themes in America during the period from 1810 to 1840."

"Sounds right up my alley, Jen," Kyle sighed as he began to yawn.

Glancing about, as they were walking to their seats, Jennifer noticed several other students yawning.

Kyle then turned down the lights as Professor Moore began her slide presentation of the examples.

"Thank you, Mr. Sheridan. Listen up, young people!" stated Professor Moore with a voice of authority. "With the discovery of the lost city of Pompeii at the beginning of the nineteenth century, Europeans were reintroduced to the classical Greek and Roman artifacts that had been buried for nearly seventeen centuries."

Continuing, she said, "Most of the enthusiasm about the classical designs had been picked up in America by artists, craftsmen, and designers. Furniture, fashion material, and wallpaper coverings soon began to reflect the classical motifs in the early part of the nineteenth century."

Kyle awoke enough to notice how several of the house plans that were now being discussed in detail resembled the house he remembered growing up in as a child. He took notice that the Georgian-style house with its symmetrical all-brick layout, small-pane windows, handsome wood moldings and mantels also attracted his parents twenty-five years ago. The house was in the Washington, D.C., subdivision of Rose Hill. That was in the northwest section of the Capitol.

"Jen," he whispered. "That's the kind of house I grew up in as a boy."

"It's really quite a handsome design. Your parents had good taste."

"And money at that point," he replied with some sense of remorse. Friday's fifty-minute class session came to a close with Professor Moore's homework assignment. "This campus is fortunately located in a region that was built during the Georgian period. Quite a few of these farmhouses and in-town residences exhibit a host of Georgian-style features."

With another burst of enthusiasm, Ms. Moore gleefully expounded, "As students of architecture, I naturally expect you to traverse the nearby countryside this weekend. Please make notes or photographic images of details that show the classical influences right here within our own environs. Come back Monday with your pictures and tales of the wonderful descriptions of all the properties you were able to locate."

Kyle looked at Jen, rolled his eyes, and said, "Naturally."

When the hall bell finally rang, Ms. Moore said, "Good luck. That's all for today. Thank you for your attention."

With some gentle nudges, Jen revived her sleepy Kyle enough to get him out of the classroom and over to the student union for breakfast. Once there, she reviewed her extensive notes. They had to laugh at Kyle's fairly blank notebook.

"And to think you're a grad student!" she said, shaking her head.

"I . . . wouldn't be if it wasn't for you, Jen . . . I love you. Here, kiss me."

"Behave. People are staring. Drink your coffee."

Two weeks from now, on September 30, Kyle Sheridan will turn twenty-three. He felt that his life was on course and that his graduate degree requirements should be completed by Christmas. He was hoping that this degree will enable him to obtain a decent-paying job.

Kyle stood nearly six feet tall, weighed 175 pounds, and had a great physique. His tuft of black hair usually remained combed and parted to the right. Kyle's handsome chiseled features and his clean-cut all-American boyish look complemented his body-building efforts. He was pleased with his recent upper-torso development.

He began regular visits to the workout room in the college gym last month. Surrounded by the campus jocks, he pushed himself to stay competitive with them.

Graduate school afforded him a schedule that most underclassmen would envy. Besides attending classes and writing on his thesis, he regularly worked alongside various professors in their offices, helping them prepare for class. For this assistant status, he received a stipend every two weeks. It wasn't much money, but it allowed him to live off campus in a small furnished attic apartment.

Kyle continued to drive his yellow late-model Mustang that had been stored in his grandparents' garage. The 1969 Shelby fastback GT was a real collector's item with its 350 CID horse-powered engine. The Mustang had been his eighteenth birthday present.

Kyle, by this point in his life, began to seriously question a lot of the information that he had received as a child. He was raised as a Christian and considered himself as honest and sincere when people asked his advice or assistance. He trusted nearly everyone and, up to now, never had any real need to question his family's integrity when it came to questions about his growing-up years.

What started his renewed interest in his upbringing began when he recently met twenty-three-year-old Jennifer Howser. She was already enrolled at Farnsworth College. Kyle came to Farnsworth after completing his undergraduate studies at state college in Pennsylvania. He and Jen were now enrolled in the same graduate studies program at Farnsworth. Last year, as seniors, they separately had taken an elective class in anthropology. Questions about their ancestors arose when Jennifer admitted to her classmates, and recently to Kyle, that she had been adopted at eleven months. She never really knew her birth parents.

Kyle, on the other hand, knew both his parents and grandparents. But after a bizarre chain of events when he was five, young Kyle was taken in and raised by his father's parents, Mary and Richard Sheridan, Sr. Together, they told elaborated stories about Kyle's evil mother, Suzanne, while, on the other hand, his father, JP Sheridan, was their idealistically perfect son.

Gettysburg, Pennsylvania
Late spring 1969

Mary Sheridan arrived home after another day of teaching senior English literature. She opened the mailbox near the front door and found a letter addressed to her youngest son, John Paul. Noticing it was from the regional draft office, her suspicions of him leaving for military service was finally realized. She felt anxious for him since his brother had already gotten his deferment and was attending nearby Farnsworth College full time as a freshman day student.

Shortly, her husband, Richard, Sr., arrived in his pickup truck and appeared somewhat agitated by his tone of voice as he slammed the truck's door. "Those new hires are the laziest bunch I've ever had to deal with! They don't know dip about construction."

"I'm sorry, darling, they just need some more time to learn your ways of management."

"They better or they'll be gone." After getting a beer from the fridge, he said, "Anything you need?"

"No, dear. I'm fine. JP got his draft notice today."

"Good! Maybe the military will deal with him better than I can!" he told her after popping the top and guzzling the entire can of beer in front of his wife.

"I don't know. I'm worried about him. He's not at all like his brother."

"That's for damn sure," he replied after belching loudly. "I'll take another beer," he said while handing her the empty can.

Mary turned, entered the kitchen, got her husband another beer, and began setting the table for dinner. She laid her son's letter by her plate and opened the refrigerator for dinner ideas.

"Hi, Mom and Pop," said Ricky, Jr., as he opened the front screened door and tossed his books and athletic gear on the sofa.

"Darling, those things go up to your room, not dumped on my sofa. Dinner will be ready soon. Go and get cleaned up and tell your pop to do the same."

"Yeah, Mom," replied her athletic nineteen-year-old jock. "Where's JP?"

"He should be home soon. He told me this morning that he was going over to Melanie's house after school."

"Probably to get some," Ricky mumbled as he climbed the steps to his bedroom with his hands full.

"What was that comment? I didn't hear you."

Upon entering his bedroom, Ricky walked past his jammed-full trophy cabinet and opened his closet. Reaching around the top shelf, he located a small metal can and set it on his desk. Opening it, he smiled, rolled, and lit up a joint. Turning around, he pushed the button on his music player and began to daydream.

Eighteen-year-old high school senior, JP Sheridan soon returned home and joined the family at the dinner table. Before beginning the prayer of thanks, Mary handed her son the letter.

"What's this, Mom?"

"It's from your Uncle Sam," his pop said with a snicker.

"Mom, I'm being drafted into the frigging army!"

"JP, your father and I are very proud of you."

"Yeah," he sighed, "what about my going to college with Suzanne? Ricky and Melanie are almost finished with their freshman year. She and I are getting ready to graduate in a few weeks, and now I have to report in thirty days to Fort Bragg, North Carolina!"

"God has other plans for you right now. Some things will have to wait. Sweet Suzanne will. You'll get there in due time," replied his mother.

"Dude, listen to me," Ricky smirked. "The army needs your help right now, and we all will support you."

"Yeah," he said, looking rather forlorn.

Following dinner, JP phoned Suzanne to give her the bad news about his scheduled new military career. She seemed not nearly upset as he was. This gave JP a weird feeling, almost as if she was expecting it. She told him to be strong and that she'll be there for him, no matter what.

Later that night, after his parents had retired, JP overheard Ricky telling another of his girlfriends, Kiki, about his brother's draft notice. Ricky left the house and drove off somewhere into the late night. J. P then returned downstairs to watch the 11:00 p.m. news.

More and more United States troops were being called up to serve in Southeast Asia, and to this point, nothing had seemed alarming owing to reported light casualties in skirmishes around the capital of Saigon. Then it dawned on him that he may be called to serve there, and that was a bit disconcerting. He retired to his room, for tomorrow was another school day, and he had better be alert in his mom's literature class . . . Or else.

Prior to turning in, JP opened the folder that contained his recent graduation photos in cap and gown. They showed him with shoulder-length hair and neatly trimmed sideburns. He now wondered how different he would look next month with a shaved recruit's haircut and a newly issued army uniform.

5

The anthropology lessons opened Kyle Sheridan's eyes as to how the experts research historic records in court house files and cemetery tombstones. Jen and he realized their pasts were merely fabricated stories about people they either never knew or only briefly remembered as children. This need-to-know became more of an issue recently when Jen informed Kyle that she was pregnant.

Beginning in December 1971 through the early part of 1973, Master Sergeant JP Sheridan obediently followed every order generated by the army's Colonel Travis Cummings, MD. Following Farnsworth's chemistry professor Henry Prestol's mysterious disappearance in late June 1972, Dr. Cummings resumed full-scale manufacturing and distributing of the newly formulated drug Sernyl.

Each assignment for JP involved more and more exchanges for hallucinogenic drugs. These drugs of choice were being manufactured daily in Farnsworth College's chemistry department. All of the money for the raw materials came from drug sales and an endless supply of Army Medical Research grants.

Both Colonel Cummings and former professor Prestol had agreed to split the profits. JP was also promised a cut of the action. He was constantly reminded of his important position to finding buyers among the six regional colleges and the two state universities.

JP lived comfortably in a small furnished suite within the confines of Fort Douglas. He was under twenty-four-hour surveillance. His every move was closely monitored by the colonel's staff. He had no recollection of his previous days' activities. Each night, he was required to attend a military debriefing.

While there, he was again subjected to mind-conditioning drugs.

Colonel Cummings and the late Professor Prestol were able to amass huge stockpiles of drugs since the government wanted more medical research done to counteract the effects of the chemical Agent Orange. Returning Vietnam veterans complained constantly of illness that they attributed to this Agent Orange. Numerous lawsuits loomed in the near future if the government did not react swiftly regarding this issue.

Master Sergeant JP Sheridan maintained his professional military appearance and outwardly acted as a dedicated young career noncommissioned officer. Everyone on base respected him for his outstanding Vietnam record.

JP's uniform proudly displayed his Purple Heart and his meritorious commendations. Many had been awarded by the colonel himself.

Gettysburg College
February 1973

"That's him. He fits this description, over there standing outside the coffee shop," said the Pennsylvania State policeman to his colleague. "Come on. We'll take him in for questioning."

The two officers, wearing civilian clothes and with weapons drawn, approached JP. He was apprehended without incident. Then he was handcuffed and ushered quietly into the backseat of the officer's car. The vehicle sped off and took its prisoner into the town's police headquarters.

After being placed into a tiny holding cell, JP was ordered to be strip-searched. The two brawny officers went through JP's clothing and recovered his military ID, several bottles of Sernyl pills, along with several thousand dollars in cash.

"Well, soldier boy. Do we have an interesting night ahead for you!"

JP frowned and tried to pull away as he was being cavity-searched. He was briefly released and pushed to the rough concrete floor. Each officer then unbuckled their heavy leather belts and together lifted their naked handcuffed prisoner up and reattached his arms to an overhead pipe.

With the heavy metal door closed behind them, the two sadistic men beat, flogged, and punched their victim with their belts and fists. JP had never experienced such intense pain and became horse from screaming.

Once they tired, the officers retreated to their office and divided both the cash and the drugs. The one officer sent a report by fax to the local newspaper while the other unhooked his unresponsive prisoner. After gathering up his clothes and personal belongings, the patrolmen tossed their prisoner into the patrol car's trunk.

Within the hour, they arrived at the main gate of Fort Douglas. The two state police talked to the army sentry and requested that their prisoner would be taken into military custody. Soon a group of military police arrived, and the prisoner exchange took place. The state police advised the MPs that their prisoner was suspected of selling drugs and should be court-martialed.

JP, still unconscious and naked, was taken to the base brig and then subjected to further abuse that night by the MPs. By dawn, his bruised and bleeding body was once again injected with a syringe and returned to the research facility. Hours later, once he was conscious, he was debriefed by Colonel Cummings and Dr. Gray.

"What you did, Sergeant, was a stupid thing. You have cost us valuable time. My shipment that was confiscated by the state troopers had a street value of over ten thousand dollars. Your termination from my program is a certainty.

Dr. Gray, secure this prisoner and have the MPs take him to the base brig."

Dr. Gray assisted JP into a fatigue-colored jumpsuit and slipped his military ID into the top pocket. He then attached ankle bracelets along with a waist chain belt. JP offered no resistance to being shackled hands and feet.

His head hung down as Dr. Gray closed the lab door and began to lead him upstairs.

Unexpectedly, Dr. Gray whispered to JP, "The key is in your right pocket.

Once you're free, overpower the guard and escape. You will not survive in the brig, I assure you."

After arriving topside, the doctor and his former patient walked slowly down the corridor to the waiting escort. The MP led JP outside into the bright and cold February sunlight. He pushed his prisoner into the backseat of the vehicle. The brawny security guard sat in the front seat and drove away. The research lab was several miles from both Fort Douglas and Farnsworth College.

JP fumbled through his jumpsuit and found the key. The driver was on a two-way radio talking to a brig staffer about some new interrogation techniques being introduced to brig prisoners. What JP heard scared him and made him more determined. Once he had unlocked the leg and wrist cuffs, he noticed the car approaching a thickly wooded area. He quickly wrapped his belt chain around the neck of the driver. The driver slumped forward, and the car began to accelerate but JP grabbed the steering wheel.

JP managed to open the driver's door and pushed the dead man out.

Jumping into the driver's seat, he was able to apply the brakes in time to stop the car. His heart was racing and his breathing was very rapid. He had not killed a man in cold blood since Vietnam. Soon, he regained his composure.

He turned the car around and drove back to where the driver's body lay in a ditch along the isolated country road. He opened the trunk and placed the body into it. After closing the lid and finding his bearings, he knew of a nearby quarry lake.

Within fifteen minutes, he stood on an old service road that led down to the quarry. Putting the car in neutral, he stood by silently and watched the military vehicle disappear into the lake.

Within a short time, JP observed two military Huey-type choppers circling behind where he had just been. He was now looking through a west coast mirror of a rig that had just picked up this hitch-hiker in a fatigue jumpsuit.

Our fugitive was now headed south toward Washington, D.C. Time seemed to finally melt away. He relaxed briefly and began to tell the truck driver, "I'm a Vietnam veteran who's trying to escape my past yet afraid of my future." Then thoughts of Melanie Dulane enter his head. "I once loved this beautiful girl named Melanie. But once I got drafted into the army, my older brother, Ricky, stole her away. Now they're both gone."

The driver listened and felt compassion for his passenger. Even though he had given rides to many other college-aged guys, each one told him stories that were quite similar. "You fellows sure know how to find love, fuck things up big time, and lose it easily. You may want to work with a good shrink about your relationships."

JP grinned, thinking how Dr. Gray had helped him escape from Colonel Cummings. Now, he was broke and couldn't find his damn steamer trunk.

6

**Georgetown
Washington, D.C.
February 1973**

Master Sergeant JP Sheridan slowly walked along M Street just before the dawn. Stars still twinkled, and a crescent moon was rapidly setting in the western sky. It hadn't snowed yet, but everyone was anticipating a white Valentine's Day because of an approaching storm front from the Ohio Valley.

Since December 1971, JP had been secretly conditioned to handle his late brother's never-ceasing list of connectors for Colonel Cummings's constant drug sales. After having been recently stung and nearly killed, he escaped yesterday and was able to hitch-hike to here.

Thoughts constantly flooded into his brain. He heard voices, had different emotion responses than he would have normally. He pictured Ricky's death, at twenty-two, from an apparent overdose in a hippie commune. It no longer seemed a total waste but was purposeful and meaningful. He was a college senior ready to graduate in May. Although his girlfriend had just had a baby girl, Ricky ignored them for the greater cause, which was to serve the colonel and Professor Prestol.

Strangers walking past JP would see his anguish and tears but offered him no condolences. He turned his thoughts to his black steamer trunk.

"Everything I own and need right now is inside that damn footlocker, and the army says it's still lost in transit!"

Tears flowed freely as JP felt utterly helpless and in an alien world. The past three and a half years in Vietnam had been difficult enough, but it was not the training ground he needed for dealing with his present situation.

Valentine decorations hung gaily in shop windows along the nearly deserted street in the predawn cold. He truly felt alone. His buddies were all back in Vietnam. "They'll have a busy day today," he thought as he continued to think about their daily routines and the good times they had shared together.

"Soon, God, let our government wake up and bring them all home," he prayed silently.

By the way things had become over there and the intense antiwar sentiments here, it probably would not be very long. However, he needed a friend now.

JP stopped at the corner in front of an unopened drug store. Reaching into his pocket, he removed a folded piece of paper and opened it. He had arrived at the address written on the paper. Looking about, he noticed the side entrance to the upstairs apartment and proceeded to ring the doorbell.

A light was turned on behind the frosted door window, and a voice asked,

"Who's there?"

"It's JP Sheridan. I'm looking for a Mr. Frederick Howard."

The old door creaked open until the security chain stopped it. "I'm Howard. I was expecting you yesterday."

"I'm sorry." replied JP. "Please, may I come in? I've been walking most of the night."

From behind the door, the voice said, "May I see some ID?"

JP removed his military card from his wallet and passed it through the narrow opening. The door latch unfastened, and he entered the narrow hallway. "Hello, Mr. Howard."

"Huh. So you want to be an artist?"

"Yes, sir. People have told me I'm talented in that way, and I really wanted to pursue it for a long time."

"I see. Call me Freddy."

"Thanks. People call me JP."

"Follow me," replied Freddy as he ascended the stairs.

JP carried only a small overnight bag with shaving things, soap, and a toothbrush.

"Where are your things?"

"My footlocker hasn't arrived from Hong Kong yet. The army has a tracer on it, and I hope to God they find it soon. Everything I own is in that damn trunk."

"Aw. Don't worry. It'll arrive soon, and you'll have the things you need."

"Yeah, but what I really need is a new life and a fresh start."

"JP, your life here will be different and exciting. I have plenty of art patrons and painting commissions coming in from many directions. You were smart to answer my ad for an art apprentice."

"I've had a strong interest in art ever since high school."

"Good," replied Freddy. "Your room is over there. The bath is at the end of the hall."

"Where's your art studio, sir?"

"It's across the street. We'll go there in a few hours after breakfast."

"That sounds fine to me."

"Listen, JP, I'm pretty casual around here. New York City, now that's formal."

"You show your artwork in New York?"

"Yes. Last year's show was my best yet. That's one hell of a great place for artists."

"Yes. I can imagine. But for now, I'll settle for Georgetown."

"This is a good place to work. Lots of inspiration, you know."

JP turned and entered his tiny new bedroom. The single window overlooked Thirtieth Street. Removing his trench coat and uniform tie, he stretched out on a single bed with an attractive antique brass headboard. He soon drifted off to sleep.

During the following weeks, Freddy introduced JP to many local artists and craft people who lived in the Georgetown area. John let his beard and hair grow. It felt good having a mentor. He began producing several paintings each week.

He closely studied how Freddy sketched and developed a likeness from his models. Freddy was a very good portrait painter, and his new apprentice often accompanied him to sittings around town. JP took careful notes of Freddy's palette colors, the lighting of his models, his brush techniques, and most importantly, the rapport he developed with each commissioned customer.

He felt confident to let Freddy arrange settings for him. The customers, of course, only paid Freddy. JP lived on a stipend. Freddy provided him with all his art materials along with food and lodging.

JP's first commission was extremely difficult. The elderly woman insisted on wearing a full-length black velvet evening gown. She posed alongside of her shiny black baby grand piano. The combination of the black gown and its reflection in the black piano became very hard to distinguish. After a while, he stopped painting and called Freddy as the session was becoming extremely tiring for both model and artist. Freddy suggested that he use two different kinds of black paint, Mars Black for her dress and Ivory Black for the piano.

It did the trick. The woman was delighted with the outcome of the portrait.

JP knew he had a lot to learn, and with Freddy as his mentor, he would go far.

One day, in the late spring of 1973, JP arrived back at the apartment above the drug store. He opened the door and discovered that the place had been ransacked. Most of the furniture and many of his paintings were gone.

He moved toward the wall phone in the kitchen, stumbling over the remaining items that littered the floor. There was an envelope taped to the phone receiver.

He opened the envelope and found a note:

Dear JP,

My sister's taken ill, and I've gone to Phoenix. I had to sell our stuff for my plane ticket. It's been good knowing you.

Take care,
Freddy Howard

"Well I'll be damned! Just like that, he ups and leaves. What the hell am I supposed to do now?" he cried. "That bastard pawned everything I owned!"

JP now realized he needed to find some new commissions for sustenance.

He quickly put an ad together.

Successful Portrait Artist seeks commissions—reasonable rates.

Call John P. Sheridan @ 202-555-4792

He called the Washington Times classifieds department, and they told him that his ad would appear in tomorrow's edition.

Sitting around a cold and nearly empty apartment all day waiting for the phone to ring was not JP's idea of a wonderful time. He eventually had dozed off.

Shortly before 6:00 p.m., the phone rang. He quickly jumped up and grabbed the receiver. "Hello, hello! May I help you?"

The soft female voice on the other side indicated a need for a painted portrait as a gift for her parents who were soon moving to Florida.

"That's fine. No problem, ma'am," JP stated, trying not to show how anxious he was for the commission.

"I live in the Watergate Apartment House on the twelfth floor on the Potomac River side. Tomorrow afternoon will be fine. I'll be home about four."

"I'll bring sketching items for my preliminary work. Oh, by the way, I didn't get your name?"

"I'm Suzanne Hardesty. Just tell the guard at the desk I'm expecting you."

He thanked her and hung up the phone. He first felt relieved to be employed again. Then his emotions overtook him. "Could it be her?" he wondered. "The same Suzanne I had dated in high school and had met again several years ago in Hawaii?"

Tears of joy filled his face as he pondered, "God, she was a fine woman if ever there was one." He thought to himself about the short courtship, the ride to the beach, and their first tender kiss.

He remembered how he had invited her to take a moonlit walk along a deserted section of beach near Waikiki. The moonlight reflected off of her beautiful face, and he knew this was the woman of his dreams. His earlier drinking with his army buddies had made him feel totally relaxed and uninhibited. She, on the other hand, was feeling relieved that her competition was over, and her pressures were also gone.

As they started to sit down on the soft sand, JP removed his shirt for her to sit on. They watched the moon glisten on the water, which made the evening feel so romantic. Soon, the young couple embraced. Throwing thoughts of life's future difficulties and situations aside, they passionately kissed and lay back onto the soft sand. Now clusters of bright stars combined with the moonlight drenched their naked bodies in a soft warm light.

Feelings of love surfaced from each of them as he gently kissed and caressed her, bringing out her own hidden passions.

Their midnight foreplay and kissing allowed him to easily access her. She cried out as he went where no man had gone before. She couldn't have found a more perfect lover. He was for her what she had longed for. He held back as long as he could until they arrived simultaneously at a climax.

They soon parted with thoughts of that special evening, never to escape their memories.

Clinging to the hope and anticipating a reunion of newfound love that next afternoon, JP walked along the banks of the Potomac River. He carried a sketch pad, charcoal sticks, and Hawaiian memories. He stopped long enough to sketch several young children playing in a playground and even a dog running and catching a Frisbee.

The April afternoon was full of the sweet fragrance of the blossoming cherry trees that lined the walkway. His watch indicated his appointment was drawing near. Ahead of him stretched the newly constructed Watergate Apartment complex. The curving of the building made this immense gray box blend with the curve of the Potomac River.

JP had become a nervous wreck. He wondered since yesterday how she would feel about their reunion. Would she reject him outright because of another lover's passion? Or would she welcome him back into her arms as a lost love? He became overwhelmed at the prospect of rejection.

Pulling himself back to the reality of his commission, he figured fate had brought him this far and would not abandon him on her doorstep. Soon the elevator doors opened onto the twelfth-floor corridor. It was a long walk down the curving hallway, which gave him more time to compose himself before he located the apartment number and rang the chime.

When the door opened, he could not have been more surprised. He stood there with his mouth open.

"Corporal JP Sheridan?"

"Suzanne Hardesty!"

After nearly three years, their eyes met once more. She raised her hands to her mouth, not knowing whether to shout or cry.

"Hello, Suzanne. It's really me. I left the army when my older brother died last November. I have worked as an itinerant portrait painter ever since then."

"Oh, JP! How glad I am to see you again. I'm sorry to hear of your loss."

As Suzanne began to open the door further, a tiny voice was heard saying,

"Mommy, who's that man?"

"JP, meet my son, Kyle."

Utter shock swept over him as this adorable little boy with blue eyes and black hair extended a tiny hand forward.

"Kyle, dearest. This is Mr. Sheridan. He's a friend of Mommy's from a long time ago."

"Hello, Kyle. I'm delighted to meet you."

"Mommy! Can he see my room?"

"Kyle! I'd love to if it's okay with your mommy."

"Be my guest," she chuckled as little Kyle led JP by the hand into his bedroom. "May I fix us a drink?" she called as they disappeared behind the wall partition.

"That's fine with me. We won't be long."

Kyle proceeded to show his guest his collection of stuffed animals, mechanical toys, and baseball equipment. Little Kyle ran out of the bedroom, yelling, "Mommy! Mommy! He likes to plays baseball! Can we go to the park?"

"Maybe in a little while, dear. Mr. Sheridan and I need to talk for a little bit. I think your cartoons are on now. Go and watch them until Mommy's done talking."

Kyle quickly ran into the other room and switched on the television and lay on the floor.

"Oh, Suzanne, I had no idea. Whatever became of you after Hawaii? And when did you have your adorable son?"

"Well, Mr. Sheridan, I believe you had something to do with his conception that moonlit night on that beautiful deserted beach. Kyle was born nine months to the day, September 24, 1970.

"After that night, I had a difficult time emotionally with my parents and returning back to my studies. You were constantly on my mind. And when I found out that I was pregnant, my world was turned upside down."

With feelings of regret, he said, "I can only imagine what you must have gone through."

"My friend told me about an abortion clinic she had gone to after her boyfriend was killed in Vietnam. She couldn't stand the thought of raising his child."

"Oh, Suzanne!"

"My parents gave me encouragement and love to carry out the pregnancy full term, and they agreed to help me raise Kyle. Then came the cancer and their decision to go to Florida and be with their close friends and relatives."

"And now, I've come back to be with you and our son."

"Oh, JP, I've waited, hoped, and dreamed of this moment."

"Suzanne, I know things are different than when we first met. Thoughts of that night continue to repeat in my dreams. We were so young and so apparently in love."

"Are you with someone else?" she asked.

"No. No one, honest. I'm just trying to survive on the street. My apartment was emptied yesterday of all my possessions by my roommate, and now, I have no place to live and nothing but the clothes on my back. I don't even have money to buy paints and a canvas for your portrait." He turned away from her lovely face and buried his face in his hands, weeping.

She tenderly wrapped her arms around him, saying, "I'm modeling professionally full time. With my parents in Florida, I need someone to babysit Kyle while I'm working. Would you consider moving in with us?"

"Oh, Suzanne! I would be delighted to be with you again. Thank you for your offer. I accept!"

Tenderly they kissed as if sealing the agreement.

They left the apartment holding hands with Kyle, who carried his ball and glove between them, and headed for a nearby park. It was a beautiful evening.

7

Twenty-two-year-old Jennifer Howser, like Kyle Sheridan, was enrolled in Farnsworth College's 1994 graduate program in architecture. Although she worked on campus as a grad assistant, she also held a part-time position with a local engineering firm as an intern architect. Her company had just recently completed building the new Farnsworth campus library.

During the construction of the library, Jennifer talked to the company owner who was also the foreman. He agreed to take her on staff for the summer. After classes resumed in the fall, she would not return to the firm until after her December graduation.

When Kyle first laid eyes on her, something told him that she would become a perfect companion and lover. Although not very outgoing, Jennifer had maintained the Dean's List throughout her undergraduate program at Penn State. Her interest had been schooling, and not the traditional party life that Kyle preferred.

Kyle's decision to become an architectural designer took a radical and more purposeful turn once he met Jen. She was beautiful, slender, five feet six inches tall with flowing light brown hair. Wide smiles always revealed her perfect teeth. She paid close attention to her makeup, accessories, and fashions.

Truly, Jennifer was one of the most attractive of the young women on Farnsworth's campus. According to Kyle, she should have entered and won all of the beauty pageants. She only laughs at his suggestion. The longer they dated, the deeper they fell in love.

They had met this past July. Before the fall semester began in August, she had agreed to move in with him in his tiny attic apartment. Dorm living had definitely lost its appeal once you had finished your four-year degree program. Wishing to continue another year of graduate studies, Jen needed a change of scenery. When Kyle made the offer, she quickly and excitedly accepted. They commuted together about twenty minutes to campus on the days their class schedules coincided. The other times, they would return to the campus separately.

"Jen, I really need to stay around here this afternoon and complete some more stuff for Professor Hill," said Kyle.

"All right, Mr. Graduate Assistant. I'm going back to the apartment and finish our laundry. I'll pick you up about five?"

"That'll be fine. Meet me in front of the library."

The young couple affectionately kissed, and Kyle crossed the sunny street. He entered the political science ground floor entrance and proceeded to Professor Hill's office. Using his newly issued key, he unlocked the office door.

"Good afternoon, Professor Hill. I'm surprised to see you here considering the shocking news yesterday about Dean Henson's death."

"Hello, Mr. Sheridan," he replied, shaking his head. "I know. It's such a horrible thing to have happen to our beloved dean."

"Who would want to harm him? He seemed to be very well liked around here," asked an innocent Kyle.

"You just never know. Someone had a motive, and at the moment, I haven't got a clue."

"Have they identified the attacker?"

"They are working on it. The guy was crushed so bad that he had to be removed from the wreckage in pieces. I'm sure it'll be all over tonight's news."

"Yeah," replied Kyle. "The press does find out about things like that quickly. I thought I'd finish grading those test papers I started yesterday?"

"Of course, be my guest. Oh, Mr. Sheridan, when you finish grading, would you mind making some space in that back storage room? Our department chairman has more stuff to put in there next week."

"Sure, Professor. Jen won't be back until five to pick me up."

"That adjoining room has been a dumping ground for quite some time. Our department never seems to keep its file boxes in good order. Any arranging you can do will surely help. You may uncover an old file cabinet back there for additional storage use. The key is here on my desk blotter."

"No problem," Kyle said with a smile.

"I'm leaving. Just pull the door closed when you're done."

"Professor Hill, have a nice weekend."

After the professor had departed, Kyle sat at his desk and graded the remaining stacks of test papers for the next couple of hours. When he finished, he entered the rear office. The cramped little room contained many boxes of student reports and term papers stacked in piles around the room. Buried behind the boxes was the old-style wooden filing cabinet.

Without windows, the space seemed tight like a closet. Each box had dates, and the professor's names scribbled across the lids. Kyle decided to at least stack the boxes by courses or instructors, and then he would be able to access the file cabinet.

After a few minutes, five stacks had been sorted. Kyle, saw open floor space and felt he had made some headway. He then decided to check the systematic arrangement employed by his predecessors inside the old file cabinet. Finding it was locked, he returned to Professor Hill's desk.

Damn, no key here, he thought. Then he noticed a small yellow envelope under the corner of the desk blotter. Looking inside, a single key slid into his palm. "Bingo!"

Kyle returned to the ancient four-drawer file cabinet and inserted the small key. The key fit, and he heard the click. The file drawers again became accessible after what appeared to be many years of neglect. He failed to notice the faded stenciling on the side of the file cabinet, Property of U.S. Army.

Gee, these files are different from the box files, he thought.

Friday Afternoon
September 16, 1994

It appeared that the files in Kyle's possession were some sort of personnel files of former students long since graduated.

I wonder if anyone knows these are still here, he thought. Professor Hill never mentioned keeping files on students, nor did anyone else here at Farnsworth.

Upon opening the remaining file drawers, he was amazed at the number of folders. Some of the files contained just several sheets of paper while others bulged and nearly split with documents and newspaper articles.

"Man, this is really strange," he said as he gently lifted one of the folders from the drawer. Taking eight files into the other room, he began to examine each one. Carefully he emptied the contents onto the Professor's Hill's desktop.

8

File One
Farnsworth College, Administration Building
Office of the Dean
January 1970

The dean, Earl Hayward, stood up and walked away from his desk toward the door following his secretary's announcement that his guests had arrived.·

"Welcome, Professors. Please come in and have a seat."

Professor Henry Prestol, along with Professor William Gray, exchanged handshakes with the dean and sat down.

"The board has voted to grant both of you tenure and assign you, Dr.

Prestol, as department head for our chemistry department and you, Dr. Gray, as department head for our psychology department. Congratulations and well done, men!"

"Thank you, Dean Hayward," they responded collectively.

"This is a new day in the long and prestigious history of Farnsworth College. Each of you is a giant and well known for you research work. Both of you are well liked and respected on our campus and elsewhere. It is a genuine pleasure to be associated with each of you. Shall we dispense with the formalities?"

"Of course, thank you again, Earl. It's an honor for me and my astute colleague, Bill, to become your department heads," replied Henry with a smile.

"Shall we toast this new occasion?"

"By all means," said a celebratory Bill, feeling a sense of new empowerment.

Once again, the dean unlocked his private liquor cabinet, uncorked two more vintage bottles of Champagne, and poured three flutes.

"To the future of our beloved institute of higher learning," toasted the dean. The three men toasted and drank and filled several more flutes before leaving.

Once outside, the professors continued their prior discussion.

"We now can actively begin recruiting for Major Cummings," replied Bill, feeling a bit tipsy.

"And my new formula can go beyond the lab rat phase," commented Henry with a fiendish look about him. Together they followed the sidewalk and were soon greeted by several students who escorted them into Dr. Gray's office.

"We'll call the major later and thank him for his influence with the board of directors," whispered Bill to Henry.

Upon opening the door, students and other professors greeted the new campus celebrities with a round of applause, well wishes, and much success as newly elected department heads. Once the celebrants departed and they were alone, Bill phoned over to Fort Douglas as Henry picked up the extension phone to listen in.

"It is official, Major Cummings. Operation CAVE can move to the next level. Henry and I will begin tomorrow on the volunteer student list I've determined are most qualified."

"Excellent, Professor Gray, I am anxious to begin. Funds will soon be transferred once you have set up a new account."

File Two
U.S. Army Headquarters
Da Nang, Vietnam
February 1970

Private First Class JP Sheridan had been in the army since last July. He finished being schooled and had been readied for combat while training in the Special Forces. As soon as he and his fellow soldiers arrived in Vietnam, they quickly met their company commander, a youthful U.S. Army lieutenant, David Prestol. He instructed the men in his platoon that he had orders for them to move out. To eighteen-year-old JP, this whole army experience was as exciting as it was frightening. Lieutenant Prestol told his men, "We will be going on a secret mission. The classified location is across the border in Cambodia, which is a vital part of the spring offensive."

Even though Lieutenant Prestol had his men load several jeeps with explosives and night gear, none of the platoon knew neither where they were headed nor the purpose of this mission. Everyone was in a heightened state of suspense. Orders were always shouted, and the young individuals acted as a united team to follow each command. Men and machines moved quickly. JP barely had time to learn his platoon member's names before they departed. He was asked by a fellow soldier if he had a nickname. He replied, "JP," with a wide grin.

Close to sunset the following day, Lieutenant Prestol addressed his platoon.

This was done prior to them moving across a makeshift pontoon bridge that spanned the Mekong River.

"Men, listen up! On the other side of this river is Cambodia. The local government officials are having a hell of a time trying to keep the Khmer Rouge under check. The bastards have a stronghold about twelve kilometers northwest of here. We're going to destroy their little ammo dump. No one knows anything about this mission or our whereabouts. Men, this mission is vital, but we are strictly on our own.

I warn you that any resistance we encounter must be dealt with quickly and quietly."

The platoon, in full battle gear and camouflage uniforms, crossed the bridge on a moonless night. After making their way through several miles of jungle, they came to a clearing. Pausing to regroup, one of the squad members tripped a wire.

The resulting explosion literally tore the young soldier's life to pieces. JP glanced back in horror as others ran to the scene. Rifle fire crackled about them, and everyone took cover. But shooting and several grenade explosions ended suddenly in an eerie silence.

"Forward, men!" whispered Lieutenant Prestol. Within a short time, the remaining platoon was standing in front of an ancient temple. The crumbling stones at the base still supported tall graceful spires that reached heavenward.

Hundreds of stone-carved deities covered nearly every inch of the temple's facade.

"I've never seen anything so beautiful," JP said to a buddy next to him.

"Me neither. In Iowa, we just have cornfields."

Lieutenant Prestol was leading the men as they quickly entered a side portal. Several armed guards were discovered at an interior room entrance.

They were quickly shot. Explosives and wire were then brought forward.

Before the platoon departed, Lieutenant Prestol and several of his men, including JP, entered into the main part of the building. They were surprised that no other guards were around. Quickly, Lieutenant Prestol ordered,

"Carefully remove the gems from the several seated statues."

After they had pocketed the gems, Lieutenant Prestol ordered, "Men, set additional explosives."

Gunfire erupted outside, and men began shouting as the lieutenant and his party ran from the temple. Within seconds, many members of the Khmer Rouge converged and entered the front entrance of the temple. They were totting heavy armor.

From the safety of the jungle and the approaching dawn, Lieutenant Prestol hit the plunger. The ancient building rocked with the violent explosions from within. A giant fireball could be seen for miles.

The platoon ran like hell through the jungle. By daylight, Lieutenant Prestol regrouped his men near the river's bank. They maneuvered across the bridge to safety.

File Three
South Vietnam
September 1971

During the spring and summer months, Lieutenant David Prestol led his men on similar daring nighttime missions. On each mission, Corporal JP Sheridan and his buddies risked life and limb while the lieutenant always took a souvenir of the occasion. He became more and more aggressive as he plundered temples and other strongholds of valuable gems, gold, and drugs.

His stash of very precious gems was smuggled to Hong Kong where exact reproductions were made. The fake items were returned to the government in Saigon for reward cash of stolen artifacts from the national museum. The real artifacts were then smuggled from Hong Kong to New York and European dealers for top black market dollars. All of that money was then sent to the lieutenant's brother, chemistry professor Henry Prestol at Farnsworth College for safekeeping.

JP and the others never questioned the lieutenant's motives or whatever he did with the recovered antique items. Whenever the platoon moved, JP was called upon to personally guard Lieutenant David Prestol's valuables.

South Vietnam
Spring 1970

JP, having been promoted to sergeant, was invited by Lieutenant David Prestol to accompany him on a special leave in Saigon. An award ceremony would take place at the army command compound. General Westmoreland was to preside and present medals.

The streets of nighttime Saigon bristled with activity and bright neon lights. Prior to tonight's liberty, JP had been escorted into Lieutenant Prestol's private quarters. The men greeted each other with a smart salute.

"Ah, good. JP, at ease, soldier."

"Thank you, Lieutenant. What's up, sir?"

"Tonight I need you to accompany me into Saigon for a special secret meeting."

"Begging your pardon, sir. I don't understand. I wasn't scheduled for leave."

"I've made all the arrangements. The duty officer fully understands the situation."

"Very well, I'll be ready."

"Fine. Now, Sergeant, listen up! You're an honest person. I believe you can be trusted totally."

"Thank you, sir. But what does that have to do with tonight's meeting?"

"Son, over the past nine months, we have gone on many missions together.

Our platoon alone has inflicted major damage to the Viet Cong. Each of our missions resulted in some sort of setback for them. You also know that during each mission, I personally took an interest in removing objects of art and jewelry from those locations."

"Yes, Lieutenant. That did appear to be a priority for you."

"I have an older brother, chemistry professor, Dr. Henry Prestol. He is on the teaching staff at a liberal arts college named Farnsworth."

"Wow! Small world, sir. My older brother, Ricky, is a sophomore there now in the class of 1973. It's not too far from where we grew up in southern Pennsylvania."

"Excellent. Then you know where Fort Douglas is located?"

"Yes, sir. The fort is up in the mountains behind Farnsworth College."

"I've never seen the place. My brother said it was beautiful, especially in the fall."

"Correct, sir. The mountain colors are spectacular."

"My brother, Henry, had informed me that something happened last year between Farnsworth College and the U.S. Army at Fort Douglas."

"Really! Ricky has never mentioned anything like that in his letters to me."

"That fact may have been kept secret from him. He may not know anything about it. I have been sending all my spoils of war to various places for resale.

My brother at Farnsworth College is using the funds to buy into a new chemical laboratory that will have the capacity to manufacture his patented formula of a phencyclidine that he calls Sernyl."

"What the hell's that?"

"It's the Peace Pill, Angel Dust, or simply, PCP. Ask your brother. I'm damn sure he'll know all about it."

"I will, Lieutenant."

"The military has had a strong interest in using Henry's new formula of Sernyl for their ongoing medical research. They pay my brother top grant dollars for it. He tells me, if things continue as they are, that in a little while, we'll all be millionaires, and we'll never have to work again."

"That sounds complicated and kind of dangerous to me, sir."

"It's a risk, but it will amass us team members a fucking fortune."

"Very good, but what does this all have to do with me?" asked JP.

"If anything happens to me, I need you to stay in close contact with my brother."

"Why me, Lieutenant Prestol?"

"Sergeant Sheridan, I trust you completely. I've already notified my brother, Henry, about you. He'll arrange for you to be stationed at Fort Douglas when you return stateside. If you decide to work with him, you'll be well compensated."

"Sir, I really appreciate that. Then I could enroll at Farnsworth College and be close to my family and my girl."

Handing JP a sealed envelope, the lieutenant said, "Here's Henry's address. Follow these instructions closely. Our mail inspectors have already been notified that his mail is 'Official Army Business.' Meet me back here at 1900 hours."

"Certainly, sir, with pleasure," JP said, smiling as he saluted and left.

9

File Four
Border Crossing between South Vietnam and Cambodia
December 20, 1970

Two unidentified wounded soldiers were being airlifted from the jungle on a chopper. Soldiers from an army platoon had assisted their wounded comrades onto the chopper. Once airborne, the chopper maneuvered between steep mountains and then proceeded in a southeasterly direction over endless stretches of rice paddies next to the open plains.

U.S. Army Hospital
Long Bihn, South Vietnam
One Week Later

The army hospital was all abuzz. When the staff car arrived, the invited press reporters quickly assembled and followed the general and his staffers into the building. Entering a medical ward, sixty-year-old General Wallace was properly saluted by the medical doctor, Major Travis Cummings, MD, a career army officer in his early thirties and a brilliant surgeon. Dr. Cummings then escorted his guests to the bedside of the two men they were honoring.

The first bedside presentation went to the twenty-eight-year-old platoon leader, Lieutenant David Prestol. The two men saluted. The general attached the Purple Heart to David's pajamas and said,

"Lieutenant Prestol, your most recent raid inflicted heavy damage to the enemy's communications. For your courage in battle and your leg injury, I am pleased to present you with this Special Forces Commendation, your Purple Heart, and your captain's insignia."

"Thank you, sir."

Flashbulbs went off as General Wallace and the new captain posed shaking hands. The general said, "We need more leaders like you around here. Well done, Captain Prestol."

He then walked to the next bed containing the twenty-year-old sergeant, John Paul Sheridan, from Sharpsville. They saluted each other, and then General Wallace attached the medals to John's pajamas saying, "This Silver Star, Purple Heart, and promotion to master sergeant are being presented to Sergeant Sheridan for rescuing Captain Prestol while suffering from his own shoulder injury. You're one hell of a soldier, young man."

"Thank you, sir. I'd do it again if I had to."

"I bet you would, son. We're very proud of what you did last week. Your folks back home will read all about it tomorrow."

Stepping out from the bedside and facing the men and the assembled press corps, General Wallace said, "Both of you men owe your lives to this talented surgeon. Guests, meet their doctor, Major Travis Cummings."

"Thank you, General Wallace. Their recovery has been excellent."

"Since I'm here, Dr. Cummings, I'll mention that your tour of duty is up, and you are being transferred to head the army's special medical research project at Fort Douglas, Maryland. Dr. Cummings, you're promotion to full colonel has also approved."

The General pinned the silver eagles on to the doctor's shirt collar. A round of applause from those in attendance was appreciated. Everyone then gave each other hand salutes.

"Thank you again, General Wallace. I appreciate your personal interest in this project."

At that point, Captain David Prestol commented, "Excuse me, Colonel.

If you recall, my older brother, Henry Prestol, is the chemistry professor at Farnsworth College and is already participating as research team members."

"Small world, Captain Prestol, isn't it?"

Sergeant Sheridan then added, "I'd say. My older brother, Ricky Sheridan, Jr., is a sophomore at that same college."

Dr. Cummings remained in the ward following the general's departure.

Doing a little eavesdropping, he listened intently as David and JP conversed, recalling past missions, recovered artifacts, and the latest mention of being required to wire all the money to his brother, Professor Henry Prestol, for safekeeping.

File Five
Honolulu Convention Center
Beauty Pageant
December 31, 1970

After the beauty pageant ended shortly after 11:00 p.m., hundreds of military personnel on leave began exiting the convention center. Many of the soldiers and sailors took taxis to the local bars and lounges. They lined the side streets in the downtown area.

Coming to Hawaii for a few days of R&R following his release from the hospital at Long Binh was just what Sergeant Sheridan needed. No missions, no choppers, and no one yelling orders for a few days were truly wonderful.

JP and several of his buddies who had also been wounded were brought here as part of their recovery procedure.

Tonight was New Year's Eve. Twenty-one-year-old JP and his buddies were ready to celebrate. The USO arranged for the tickets to a beauty pageant, and the men were not at all disappointed when they saw all those beauties lined up on the stage in their skimpy swimwear.

As JP's group entered a lush tropical restaurant and lounge around 9:00 p.m., the men noticed that several of the beauty contestants were already seated and giggling with a funny-looking gray-haired man. JP recognized one of the models. He could not believe it. It was his former high school sweetheart, Ms.

Suzanne Hardesty. She was introduced as living in Washington, D.C.

"Hey, guys. See that gorgeous blonde over there from the pageant?"

"Yeah, JP, bet you'll never get a date with her," mumbled his buddies.

"Twenty bucks each says I will."

"Damn! It'll be worth it just to see her turn your dumbass down, JP."

"Here. You all go sit there and watch how a pro does it."

JP's buddies proceeded to laugh and turn their attention to the overendowed waitress in the grass skirt. As she approached to take their drink requests, the newly decorated master sergeant casually walked over to Suzanne's table.

"Good evening, Ms. Hardesty. I'm Sergeant Sheridan from Pennsylvania.

My friends call me JP," he said with a wide grin and his arm in a sling.

Suzanne let out a glee of delight upon seeing him again. She wrapped her arms around him, and they passionately kissed.

"I really enjoyed your performance this evening."

"Oh, JP! How great to see you. These are my friends, Deloris, Judy, Tiffany, and our agent, Herbie."

"It's nice to meet you, ladies, and you too, sir."

"I'm just so delighted you army boys came to our show," Suzanne said with a beautiful white smile. "Are you alone?"

"My buddies are over there in the corner crying in their beers."

"Now why would they be doing that?"

"Let's just say they never thought I'd actually talk to you and ask you for a date, again."

"My, Sergeant, you certainly do act quickly!"

"With such a lovely model, I couldn't resist."

"Well, Sergeant. You're in luck. Come. I know a place where not even my agent can find me."

They excused themselves and quickly left the restaurant. They hailed a taxi and rode off into the night. A little while later, the taxi left them off on the leeward side of the island near a rock-strewn beach. The moon reflected on the ocean, and the warm sea breeze lifted Suzanne's long blond hair as they strolled along the secluded beach holding hands. JP felt wonderful. Even his wounded shoulder did not bother him. He was relaxed and very at ease talking to Suzanne. She was fascinated with his variety of conversational topics and felt comfortable and safe with him. Neither of them had a romantic interest back home.

JP found out a lot of interesting facts about Suzanne's modeling career and her goals since he had left for Vietnam. He cautioned her to be aware of people who would use her talents to their advantage. He then added that he wasn't that kind of guy. She told him that she hoped he was, which led to their first kiss.

As fireworks burst in the distance at midnight, Sergeant JP Sheridan fell passionately in love again with the twenty-one-year-old model Suzanne Hardesty on the sandy beach of Oahu Island.

Under the romantic moonlight, they undressed each other, and he began to stimulate her with his tender kisses and caressing. She hugged him and pulled him closer to her. He fondled her breasts, which brought on the desired effect. He suckled her hard nipples to a point where she was becoming hysterical with lust. They felt their body's temperature rise, and their hearts continued beating loudly. She pushed him far enough for her to touch his erection. He was ready to explode with anticipation. Shortly, she permitted him to enter her. Suddenly, lustful desires overwhelmed her. He was cautious at first and waited for her approval. He knew she was approaching a climax, and he wanted it to feel as wonderful for her as it was beginning to feel for him. The two arrived at simultaneous climaxes and collapsed into each other's arms, allowing their waves of passion to subside. Soon, the naked lovers began to recover enough, and he said, "Oh, Suzanne! No one has ever made me feel the way you did tonight."

"Yes. I felt your love was sincere, and I want this feeling to never end. Happy New Year, darling."

"Fate brought us back together tonight."

"And she'll unite us again soon, I hope."

They were relaxing in each other's arms when he said, "I've been bad, in a good way."

Looking concerned, she asked him, "What do you mean?"

"I'm involved in a covert military operation. I have assisted my commanding officer to recover gems and art items from the enemy's hands.

These looted objects then are given back to the government in Saigon for a reward. This extra income gets deposited into a Mercantile Bank account.

Don't tell anyone, but I'm one of the junior partners in this joint venture."

"Oh, JP! That sounds wonderful. Are you very rich?"

"The account has grown quickly. There should be enough money for my partners and myself to retire in comfort."

"Now that's what I call taking advantage of a tough war-time situation."

"There's one more thing I would like to mention, just because it's very important to me."

"Yes, please go on."

"I had to name my unborn child, if I ever have one, as heir to this account."

"And what name will this lucky child have?"

"I've always liked the Irish names, Kyle for a son, and Cathy for a daughter."

"Kyle and Cathy are names that are not too often chosen. I like them too."

After watching the sun come up, they left the beach. A taxi returned Suzanne to her hotel and then took JP back to the army base.

10

Kyle placed the documents back into the file and commented to himself, "This isn't regular college stuff. This is goddamn surveillance and spy material!" What he had read was data that had apparently been collected for a top secret army medical project. The project title was "Civilian and Army Voluntary Experiences." The code name CAVE had been referred to a hell of a lot of times. This student's folder revealed academic information, suspected and observed drug activity reports from undercover agents, sites and dates of antiwar protest participation, and newspaper clippings about an individual named Lancer, arrest and conviction for a firebombing of a local draft office in 1971, along with documents pertaining to his expulsion from campus and sentencing to the state pen for twenty-two years.

File Six

Throughout the years of 1970 through 1972, Ricky Sheridan, Jr., obediently followed every order generated by army Colonel Cummings and Farnsworth's chemistry professor Henry Prestol. Each assignment involved more and more exchanges for newly generated hallucinogenic drugs. The drugs were being manufactured daily at Farnsworth College's chemistry department and the money for the raw materials came from the Army Medical Research grants.

Both Colonel Cummings and Professor Prestol agreed to split the profits.

Ricky was also promised a cut of the action. He was constantly reminded of his important position to finding buyers among the six regional colleges and state universities.

Ricky lived comfortably in a small furnished motel suite between the campus and Fort Douglas. He was under twenty-four-hour surveillance. His every move was closely monitored by the colonel's staff. He had no recollection of his previous days' activities. Each night he was required to attend a military-style debriefing. While there, he was again subjected to mind-conditioning drugs.

Colonel Cummings and Professor Prestol were able to amass huge stockpiles of drugs with the endless supply of money. The government wanted medical research done to counteract the effects of the chemical Agent Orange. Returning Vietnam veterans complained constantly of illness that they attributed to this Agent Orange. Numerous lawsuits loomed in the near future if the government did not react swiftly regarding this issue.

Ricky maintained his hippie appearance and outwardly acted as a celebrity cultural icon. As a major supplier of drugs, he was very popular on each campus he visited.

Regional Draft Office
Ambersburg, Pennsylvania
September 12, 1972

The evening rain was pouring down. No one noticed the older yellow 1969 Mustang parked behind the two-story brick building. Two young white males ran from the car into the alley between the buildings. They hid from the streetlights under an awning canopy. Both men were carrying items of destruction. Teddy Lancer had a crowbar and a flashlight while his accomplice, Ricky Sheridan, carried gasoline-filled bottles and some old rags.

They forced their way into the Recruitment Office and Selective Service Headquarters and began to ransack the offices. As they fumbled around in the darkness, they discovered that many filing cabinets contained entire draft records of all the regional high school male students who were eighteen years old.

Their bottles ignited into flames as they finally lit their Molotov cocktails.

The two rooms of bureaucratic paperwork quickly became engulfed in flames.

They barely escaped alive into the rainy night. The heat was tremendous.

They quickly drove off as fire alarms began to ring. It was a daring mission, but they were experienced in this technique.

The following day, everyone at Farnsworth College read all about the daring nighttime raid. Even the two students who carried out the assault read about it.

Thirty-five-year-old chemistry professor Henry V. Prestol, sporting his goatee, thick-rimmed glasses, and blue lab coat, entered his office and addressed the two perpetrators of the crime. "What you boys did last night was very commendable. The recruiters will have to find new headquarters, and when they do, we'll be back. Now, listen up, you two."

Professor Prestol began detailing the planned activities for the next several weeks. They included another draft office break-in, a major antiwar protest in Washington, and assisting several more draft-dodging friends of his to reach Canada by using their established underground network.

"My time is now divided between teaching here on campus and doing chemical research for Lieutenant Colonel Cummings at Fort Douglas. I've heard, through the grapevine, that our army buddies are moving into a new research phase because so many returning GIs complained of being poisoned by inhaling the defoliant Agent Orange. I will probably need both of you to manage my drug distribution here and at the other area colleges. My efforts, with your help of course, have made me a modern-day drug czar."

"How will this change affect us, Professor?" asked Teddy.

"Arrangements will be made, and the two of you will be very busy."

"Sounds good to me," explained Ricky.

"Me too," said Teddy.

As the professor and his accomplices left his office, another student named Joey Henson made a call from the pay phone in the corridor. After depositing the dime, he said, "Hello, I have a message for Lieutenant Colonel Cummings.

The clock is ticking, and the authorities will be notified. That's all. Thanks."

Joey then boldly called the Pennsylvania State Police Headquarters in Ambersburg and implicated his friend and Farnsworth College student Teddy Lancer as the arsonist in yesterday's draft office fire.

Within several hours, Teddy was taken into custody and jailed on five-hundred-thousand-dollar bond. Unable to get either Professor Prestol or Joey Henson's help, he quickly was convicted and sentenced to twenty-two years in the Pennsylvania State Penitentiary near Pittsburg.

"Man. This is some story. This poor son of a bitch did it all and paid dearly," Kyle said out loud to the empty dimly lit room. A photocopy of a Pennsylvania driver's record was also found among the pages. Being so consumed with the information contained in this single file, Kyle failed to notice the time.

"Gosh! Look at the time, 5:30 p.m.! Jen will be so upset."

He returned the file folder, closed the cabinet, and decided to put the key on to his key ring. Closing the office door, he ran down the empty corridor and outside, waving to Jennifer who looked tired of waiting.

Unknown to Kyle, a solitary figure emerged from a nearby out-cove and unlocked and entered Professor Hill's office. The figure picked up and dialed the phone saying, "The mouse has taken some bait."

"Where the hell have you been?" Jen scolded Kyle. "I've been sitting here for almost forty-five minutes!"

"I'm sorry, babe. Really I am."

"What's your excuse? It couldn't be that you were studying nor doing some research pertaining to our weekend assignment."

"I don't know."

"What don't you know?" she inquired, being surprised at his answer.

"I was cleaning up some boxes in the storage room that adjoined Professor Hill's office, and I came across an old file cabinet. The professor told me it was there buried under boxes."

Jennifer started the car and drove them off campus. "Go on with your excuse. Why you were late?"

"Well, earlier on, Professor Hill mentioned the location of the key to the files. I did locate the key and opened the old cabinet. It appeared to contain hundreds of files on student activities from the late 1960s and early 1970s."

"Huh. Did you snoop?"

"I spent two hours reading about one particular student named Teddy Lancer, class of 1973. It was fascinating—antiwar protests, drugs, hippies, and secret surveillance information."

"Really!"

"And guess what?"

"He slept with the female dean?" Jennifer said sarcastically.

"No, something a hell of a lot hotter than that! This guy was immediately sentenced to twenty-two years in jail for firebombing a draft office in Ambersburg back in 1972."

"Interesting," she replied wide-eyed. "Please pick up a newspaper tonight so we can read all about Dean Henson's assassination."

That same Friday afternoon, recently released from the military prison at Fort Leavenworth, Kansas, Dr. Travis Cummings, MD, entered Farnsworth College's administration building. He made his way through the familiar settings. Upon reaching the third floor, he entered an office down the hall from the corner office of the late dean, Joseph Henson. That office had been cordoned off as a designated crime scene with yellow tape. The acting dean, Dr. Thomas Witherspoon, PhD, along with Professors Moore and Hill were already seated around a conference table.

"Welcome back, Dr. Cummings. It's been a long time since you've paid a visit here. We're pleased you could join us," said Dr. Witherspoon.

"Hmmm, but thank you all. May I be the first to announce your full-time appointment as Farnsworth's new dean?" replied the doctor.

Dr. Witherspoon, acting surprised, said, "That's an honor I didn't expect."

"Well, with all the negative publicity Henson's murder generated, we needed a solid spokesman."

"He's right, you know," commented Professor Moore.

"Congratulations, Thomas."

"You have my vote too," added Professor Hill.

"Thank you all, I accept. Oh, by the way, the doctor, once again yesterday, had brilliantly demonstrated another exceptional CAVE operation by taking out both Dean Henson and Ted Lancer simultaneously."

With a modest grin, the doctor replied, "SOP, you know, standard operating procedure. Thank you, Dean Witherspoon." Continuing, the doctor said, "Now, gentlemen, ma'am, I've been waiting twenty long years. And with that wimp Henson out of the way, things should progress as scheduled. Professor Hill, you also are to be congratulated. Your description of the lad Kyle Sheridan was accurate. He's the one all right. Looks just like his old man, JP, too."

"The bait already has been taken," Professor Roger Hill informed everyone.

"And here, Doctor, is Kyle Sheridan's fingerprint lifted from my slide box," said Professor Moore as she handed him a piece of clear tape.

"Excellent work, both of you," Dr. Cummings replied with an evil smile.

Usually, their evening would be spent doing some early-semester research for their recently assigned graduate thesis or some other term papers that would soon be due. Lately, Kyle seemed to have become quite an exhibitionist with Jen's approval. He spent much of his apartment dwelling time parading around only wearing his white Jockey briefs.

He told Jen, "I'm constantly warm for one reason or another."

She, having just recently learned about her pregnancy, didn't seem to mind admiring his well-developed physique. In fact, she would often move in behind him quietly and slide his briefs down. After arousing him and tenderly positioning a condom, they enjoyed together what became long and fulfilled sexual encounters.

He also told her that these sexual acts allowed him to remain focused on his mission to get through this demanding graduate study program. This caused Jennifer to laugh more and call him My Mr. Horny.

Later that evening, Kyle read in utter disbelief that the individual accused of murdering Dean Henson was named Ted Lancer, the same person's file he had just read about in Professor Hill's old cabinet.

The Gazette headlines echoed a suspicious community's shock by stating, "Many unanswered questions about the secret and unethical practices at Farnsworth College today and that of nearly twenty-five years ago are being raised again."

"They were all students together!" exclaimed Kyle. "Listen to this. This dude, Lancer, in the class of 1972, was recently released this week from the state penitentiary near Pittsburgh and was listed as formerly residing outside of Harrisburg. His return yesterday to the Farnsworth campus was apparently to settle an old score with the college's dean, Dr. Joseph Henson. Both men knew each other and were considered campus radicals during the turbulent early 1970s."

"Such a coincidence that the creep was actually on our campus yesterday morning. And now you're reading about his shady past life this afternoon and this evening."

Kyle continued reading the newspaper saying, "Mr. Lancer's death was a result of him using an unstable fire escape to flee the third-floor window of the dean's office. Sources reported that the wall-hung brackets apparently broke, and his weight caused it to collapse and kill him. Dr. Thomas Witherspoon, the acting dean, will deliver a eulogy at Farnsworth's chapel on Sunday afternoon at two."

"Funny how someone using the fire escapes would get killed when it broke," Jen stated.

"I thought this county's fire marshal would have people who would inspect things like that regularly."

"They do."

"Naw, that couldn't be," he replied with an air of skepticism.

"What couldn't be, dear?"

"Jen, do you suppose that Dean Henson expected this guy Lancer to visit and had actually tampered with the fire escape, which caused it to fall?"

"Kyle, dearest, this whole mess isn't any of our concern. These men were as old as our parents and came from a different era with different values and their own problems."

"You're right. Let's focus on house hunting tomorrow for our class assignment."

Kyle led Jen into the tiny bedroom, and after another hour of lovemaking by the romantic light of the television, they fell asleep in each other's arms.

11

Day Four
Saturday
September 17, 1994

Saturday morning shone brightly as Jennifer rose from Kyle's embrace and went into their tiny apartment kitchen. She turned on the TV as the coffeemaker began to drip. She stopped fixing breakfast long enough to hear a news reporter's comments.

"Media attention has again focused on the quiet and peaceful campus of Farnsworth College. Thursday, their dean, Dr. Joseph Henson, was savagely attacked and killed by a fellow alumnus Ted Lancer. Both men—"

Click.

Jen set the remote down and stared out of the window. She wondered if her deceased mother was part of the campus uprising in the early 1970s. The Howser family was chosen to adopt her when she was eleven months old. They had woven a tale of mystery about her real mother. All Jennifer knew was that her true mom was a drugged-out hippie girl named Melanie and that she had been a student at Farnsworth College in the late 1960s. She was a Flower Child, a drug user, and was pregnant by her live-in boyfriend. The boyfriend, through a drug overdose, died when Melanie's baby girl was nine months old. Jennifer's life hung in jeopardy when her hippie mom was committed to a mental hospital and she was placed into foster care. "How terrible it must have been for my young mother," Jen sighed.

The Howsers had no children when they adopted eighteen-month-old Jennifer. Instantly she became the center of their love. After their deaths, Jen, with her inheritance and her scholarships, was able to attend Penn State. She felt strangely attracted to the smaller and seemingly friendlier Farnsworth College for her advanced degree. Although she just recently met Kyle, they fell totally in love.

She eagerly accepted Kyle's invitation to move into his off-campus apartment. The tiny apartment was full of sketches and other class projects. They were both gifted in designing architecture and both had well-developed mathematical abilities. Together they worked on conceptual illustrations and small-scale models of their design structures.

Kyle leaned toward commercial concepts and liked submitting plans for malls, sport complexes, and even school buildings. Jen preferred custom homes. She thought that when she would become a certificated architect, she would enjoy working with individual homeowners, and not commercial corporations as Kyle did. She drew a lot of inspiration from her favorite early-twentieth-century American architect Frank Lloyd Wright. Jen loved how he was able to design furniture for the inside of his homes. According to her instructors, she also exhibited flair in that field.

As a graduate assistant, Kyle worked in several departments on campus. He liked the variety of assignments because they gave him more income and experiences. One other thing they had in common was that they were both born in 1970.

Jen now moved into the living room and sat on the sofa staring out of the window. Today was Saturday, and it was shaping up to be a lovely, cool September morning. Her thoughts bounced between Thursday's crime scene on campus and the day she was told of her adopted parent's death in an automobile accident caused by a drunk driver crossing the median. She, fortunately, had opted not to go with them that day. That simple decision had saved her life.

Jen had worked hard to overcome her personal loss. After meeting her sexy and romantic Kyle, she discovered that his life was also filled with some traumatic events and unanswered questions. She didn't know all the details about Kyle's experiences and never wanted to upset him with prying questions. She felt special when occasionally he would voluntarily talk to her about his past life. She knew that discovering those files yesterday seemed very important to Kyle. She thought, Perhaps, somewhere out there, he'll find another piece of our personal history puzzles.

"Darling, where are you?" came from the bedroom.

"Here on the sofa having a coffee."

The bedroom doorway soon filled with her muscular hero wearing his white Jockey briefs and yawning.

"Good morning, Kyle. I really enjoyed last night. You were so intense."

"Baby, put that coffee cup down and give me a morning hug right now."

Her heart began to beat faster as she moved toward him. His touch and embrace were overpowering. She melted in his strong arms as he gently lifted her off of her feet. He carried her back onto the bed. His hands slowly removed her robe, and she slid his briefs down. The moments following were as intense as last night.

After recuperating, Jen said, "Kyle, I think we should spend some time this afternoon on our class assignment."

He rolled over and pretended to return to sleep, but she insisted, so he revived, got up, and proceeded to shower. She entered the bathroom as he kissed her and got dressed. She, after dressing and fixing her hair, prepared her lover something to eat.

Following lunch, Kyle and Jen got into his '69 Mustang and drove back toward the campus. Kyle said, "This county road map showed quite a number of isolated farmhouses near the college. Maybe that will be a good place to start."

Seeing a turnoff, Kyle drove slowly down the narrow road until he came to a fork in the road.

"This heritage trail seems to go to the right, dearest."

"Take a look over there on that hilltop," she said while pointing in that direction.

"That's some beautiful house."

"Do you think it is what we're looking for?" he asked.

"Not, exactly. It's too modern. It looks early-twentieth century if you ask me."

"But look beyond that one at that old dilapidated place over by the bridge."

"Huh. From here, the stone house does look very symmetrical."

"That's a good sign," he said.

As they drove closer, the old two-story farmhouse appeared to be at least 150-plus years old. Being abandoned and covered with wildly growing vines, the stone structure beckoned to be explored. Kyle parked the car off of the road. Then they walked slowly up the overgrown path to the house.

"Be careful of the briers and thorns," Kyle warned her.

"I'll be all right, thanks."

When they finally stood in front of the once-beautiful facade, they observed specific architectural features as the sunlight bounced off of the stones, the freeze board, and the cornice, creating interesting shadows.

"Kyle, look up there on the overhang. There's evidence of a classical motif in the cornice molding."

Shading his eyes and squinting, he commented, "Yes, I see it. All hand carved, I bet."

"See the lintels over the windows and the door? They too must have been hand carved."

"It's a damn shame the owners let it become so rundown."

"Do we dare look inside?" she whispered while holding tightly on to Kyle's jacket sleeve.

"This place is totally deserted. I don't think anyone would mind if we took a look around inside."

The fearless couple casually entered into the darkened interior. Immediately, the floorboards creaked under their weight. Nearly every window had been broken out.

"Oh god! It's exciting," exclaimed Jen.

They walked through one large empty room after another and saw broken plaster strewn everywhere. Some of the walls contained graffiti from ages ago. She continued looking for classical details.

"Sorry, the mantels and wainscoting are gone," sighed Kyle while looking around the formal dining room.

"Can you imagine entertaining in such a place? Our whole apartment would fit inside this one room!" exclaimed Jennifer.

They continued their tour. He held her hand tightly as they ascended the rickety stairway with its handrails missing. They walked into a paneled empty bedroom where one of the ancient wood panels was hanging loose. Opening a paneled narrow door, Jennifer found a tiny hidden stairway that led up to the attic.

"Come on, dear. This is terrific, a secret stairway."

"I . . . I don't know, darling. It could be dangerous. We might find broken or rotted wooden beams."

She fearlessly pushed cobwebs aside and led the way. Soon the couple stood upright in the narrow attic space. Some flooring was missing in places, and sunlight shone through many openings in the old roof.

"Secluded enough for you?" he asked with a gleam in his eye.

"Of course, go ahead."

He quickly removed his jacket and shirt. She moved closer, and they gently kissed. Her hands loosened his belt, and she gently tugged his Levi's downward. Her delicate fingers slid along the waistband of his white Jockey shorts, and she lowered herself down his smooth chiseled chest and stomach. He let out a soft moan as she fondled the bulge in his briefs.

Lying totally naked and relaxed on their pile of clothes strewn upon the attic floor, she said, "Kyle, what's that?" She pointed toward the corner of the room.

"Don't know. Let's take a look."

After putting his briefs back on, he carefully lifted a shallow metal box from beneath the weathered-looking floorboards.

"There's something inside, but it's locked pretty secure."

"I wonder how long it's been there?" she asked after examining the six-by-twelve-by-four-inch-deep metal box.

"It doesn't look that old, Jen, maybe twenty or thirty years, or less."

"Let's take it with us. It's been here long enough without anyone making a claim."

"Whatever you say, dearest, I think it's time we get dressed and move on."

He put the metal box in the trunk, and the couple drove off down the country lane. The afternoon remained sunny enough for them to spot several other neighboring farmhouses that appeared to be from the Georgian period and occupied. As the afternoon grew dark, the couple decided to drop by Professor's Hill office for Kyle to borrow some more files before returning home.

They had their field notes for class and the metal lockbox. They felt tired and hungry as they entered the apartment.

"Kyle, I do appreciate your helping me to get these notes for Monday. There's enough for both of our reports."

"Good for us and for Ms. Professor Moore." He laughed.

"I wonder who used to live in that old abandoned house."

"Perhaps whatever is in this box will tell us about the previous owner. I'll fool with the lock after dinner."

"Okay, I got your message. We'll be eating shortly," she replied as they held each other and gently kissed.

After dinner, he picked the lock of the metal box with a bobby pin. They were surprised at the contents. There were two folded pieces of stationary. Each had an imprint at the top of each sheet saying, "Mercantile Bank and Trust, 600 Front Street, Harrisburg, Pennsylvania." One sheet had three rectangles, two larger and one smaller inside of a larger one along with a diagonal broken line connecting the two larger boxes.

The other folded sheet had a series of numbers printed with hyphens. Much to Kyle's surprise, there was a dried-up bottle of spirit gum along with a fake Goethe and mustache.

"So who wore this disguise?" asked Kyle as he held the items to his clean-shaven face and looked into a nearby mirror.

"Very distinguished, that makes you look like a real hippie professor," she said with a chuckle.

"Right on, baby, I probably could fool a lot of people with these."

"Only if you were a good actor."

"All right, I get you point."

Jennifer began to closely examine the two sheets of faded paper. She wondered if this was a map of sorts and if the numbers were actually a combination to a locker or a safety deposit box in that bank. They talked further after he had opened another file.

12

Jen began telling Kyle, "These articles seem to be from the late 1960s. Ms. Alexander was on the facility of another college as a professor of political science for several years and became the department chairman from 1967–'69. By early spring 1970, she appeared at Farnsworth College. She must have maneuvered herself into the deanship. It also appears that she was quite powerful and used people to her advantage. Read this article." She handed it to Kyle.

File Seven
Fort Douglas
U.S. Army Base, 1970
Army Base Administration Headquarters

The newly appointed Farnsworth College dean, Tricia Alexander, was seated face to face with army lieutenant colonel Travis Cummings, MD. She was examining documents that were laid out on a conference table.

"I think this is an excellent plan, Dr. Cummings. We may encounter some resistance from internal foes who believe your secret research project too expensive and that it will drain the college's resources."

"Just remind those communists that rebuilding burned-out campus buildings would be much more expensive."

"Your outline calls for extensive medical research, student volunteers, mind conditioning, LSD experiments, and programmable campus security personnel. What are you calling this program?"

"Operation CAVE, which stands for 'civilian and army voluntary experiences.'"

After Dean Alexander signed the pact between Farnsworth College and the U.S. Army Medical Research facility at Fort Douglas, she was given a private tour of the facility by the lieutenant colonel.

A military bus unloaded a group of six civilian men in their early twenties.

An army sergeant and a lieutenant directed the recruits into a building that had a newly painted sign over the door which read "CAVE Medical Research Facility—Authorized Personnel Only."

The sergeant opened the door and said, "This way, men!"

After they had entered the building, the recruits made a line in the reception area. "Welcome aboard, men," said the young lieutenant. "Dr. William Gray will meet all of you inside shortly, and he'll explain your indoctrination procedures and answer any questions."

In another section of the building, Dr. Travis Cummings was still showing Farnsworth's dean another phase of his operations. As they entered into a dark room, he opened a draped window. Looking out into a large operating room, they saw a room that was similar to a major city's hospital operating room.

They watched as doors opened on the other side of the large room, revealing those five dissident college students, three males and two females, who were now lying unconscious.

"They are going to be carried into my secret lab by my military personnel."

"What happens next?"

"Well, Dean Alexander, these students are called Flower Children. IVs will be attached to them, and they will be subjected to various types of LSD experiments for mind control. Although absent today, my right-hand men oversee the behind-the-scenes lab work. They are Farnsworth's Professor Dr.

Henry Prestol from your chemistry lab and psychology Professor Dr. William Gray. Dr. Gray screens the volunteers first and obtains their signatures giving us their permission to enter into our drug treatment program. I keep all of the patients' files and records of their experimental progress. Special guests, such as you, may view their progress through this two-way mirrored glass window."

He tapped on the glass, and several other medical personnel on the other side of the glass looked over and gave the thumbs-up.

Kyle told Jen, "I remember overhearing Professor Hill mention to a colleague that Ms. Alexander had made many enemies after appointing certain questionable friends to high college positions."

"Kyle, it says here that she and her fiancé, a Dr. Henry Prestol, resided in a period pre-Civil-War-era stone farmhouse near Farnsworth College."

"Maybe we were inside their old house?"

"Makes sense to me."

"Whatever happened to Henry what's his name?"

"I don't know. There isn't anything else on him in these pages."

"Get a load of this article, dear."

Jen handed him a Gazette newspaper article from 1972 that showed a picture of two college individuals who were being arrested during a campus demonstration by what appeared to be military-style campus police.

"I don't believe my eyes!" he exclaimed. "That's my uncle, Ricky Sheridan, and our late Dean Henson."

"Well, it appears to me that they would have criminal records in the local police or FBI files."

"I never knew that my uncle Ricky was a member of this gang."

Ricky Sheridan, Jr., entered the chemistry lab as he had done nearly every day since he began working exclusively for Professor Henry Prestol.

"Good morning, Professor."

"Ah. Good, you're here. Come over to my desk and take a seat."

Ricky sat down as Henry lit a cigar and took some puffs. "Today things are about to change with regard to our dealing with Colonel Travis Cummings, MD."

"How is that possible, Professor?"

Henry took out a folder marked "Top Secret" and removed a single sheet of paper.

"An associate of the colonel's just brought me a photocopy of his memo. The army has just agreed to provide additional funding for the colonel's research project. I think I've discovered a way to tap into his new resources without his knowledge."

"Wow, man! Like that's totally cool, Professor."

"It won't be easy, but I'm certain, with your help, I can pull it off."

"Like how much money are we talking about, Professor?"

"Oh, several million, I'm certain, to begin with."

"But, like doesn't he have to account for all the money he spends?"

"He does, but here's the catch. I've developed a way to dilute some of the chemicals that he needs for his Sernyl experiments. It doesn't change the effectiveness of the drug, but it reduces the cost per dose to manufacturer."

"So, like, what you're telling me is you can shortchange his drugs without changing the price per dose?"

"That's it in a nutshell, Ricky."

"That way he'll pay full price, and you pocket the difference."

"That difference, as you called it, will be deposited on a regular basis in our Mercantile Bank account. My brother David's contributions from Vietnam of his recovered stolen artifacts scam will be included."

"Yeah! That's a damn good source of additional income too. Having exact reproductions made of the recovered artifacts in Hong Kong allows me to get those items smuggled to Europe for resale on the black market. My contacts there have just wired me a handsome amount."

"That's amazing, Professor."

"Yes, just as your younger brother, JP, is helping my younger brother, David, so you are helping me."

"Right on! That's what I like to see, brothers working together!"

"Go. You'll be late for class. Meet me back here after four this afternoon."

"No problem, Professor. Can you hook me up?"

"Oh, Ricky, I nearly forgot your injection."

"Thanks, man. You're a real lifesaver."

Ricky unbuttoned his cuff and rolled up his sleeve. Taking a short length of rubber tubing from the desk drawer, he made a tourniquet and balled up his fist. Henry handed him the syringe and watched as Ricky injected himself.

"That's really the good shit, Professor. Thanks. I needed that."

Waiting for the drug to take effect, Henry puffed on his cigar. "Now, Ricky, tell me again about the colonel's memo."

"What are you talking about, man? There ain't no friggin' memo that I know of."

"Good, Ricky. Go to class and I'll see you after four."

"Bye, Professor. Catch you later."

Once Ricky had left Farnsworth's chemistry lab, Henry sat at his desk and did some more calculations on an adding machine. When he finished, he smiled and tore off the paper tape. Wadding it up, he shot a basket into the nearby trash can.

"This other article," replied Kyle, "says that these three students, Joey Henson, Ricky Sheridan, and Teddy Lancer, were implicated as ring leaders in a series of campus disruptions by Ms. Alexander. It further states that following the firebombing of the regional draft office in Ambersburg on September 12, 1971, these students each was also under suspicion of the arson fire. Teddy Lancer was quickly arrested by police from an anonymous tip. He must have become the fall guy for that fire."

"Well, if my uncle Ricky was anyway involved with getting her pissed off, it could have been another explanation for his drug overdose in November 1971."

"Huh! What was the version you heard?"

"My grandma only mentioned that his hippie girlfriend had given him the tainted drugs and then she was committed to the state mental hospital in Lebanon."

Kyle and Jen spent several more hours assembling a portrayal of Ms. Alexander. The documents apparently had been kept, perhaps by her fiancé. Every item illustrated her leadership abilities and her aggressive actions. She worked hard to stifle and control any and all unrest on campus during the violent antiwar demonstrations of the early 1970s.

Evidence showed she ruled her staff and certain informers who were placed among the student body with an iron fist.

"She really used her position well to ensure that the mission of Farnsworth remained untarnished . . . until . . ."

"What?" Kyle asked with great interest.

"A federal investigation was directed to begin at Farnsworth College on June 15, 1972. This paper claims she personally impeded the investigation by stonewalling information about secret drug deals and money laundering that others claimed she was responsible for."

"Good God! That seems hard to believe that she did all of that dirty work while acting as the dean."

"Why wasn't all of that pursued?"

"It says here, 'Once the Watergate break-in hit the news on June 18, all media attention turned away from Farnsworth College and their internal problems.'"

13

**Day Five
Sunday
September 18, 1994**

The Sunday morning worship service in the nearby community of Thruville allowed Jennifer to meditate and Kyle to sleep. As she scanned the congregation, she noticed a familiar face. Following the church service, she and Kyle approached that person.

"Hello again, Dr. Cummings. Remember us?"

"Certainly, we met last Thursday in all the commotion over the dean's murder. Let's see . . . it is Kyle and Jennifer."

"Correct, sir. Hello. Nice service."

"Well, it would be if you were a true follower."

"Aren't we all on the road to salvation?" asked Jennifer.

"That's your belief, then fine. Mine is headed in another direction."

"Oh, Doctor, you mentioned the deaths at Farnsworth College back in the 1970s."

"Yes. That's true."

"Well, sir, my boyfriend and I have recently discovered information about two individuals from that time. One was that Lancer fellow who just killed Dean Henson and the other was about Dean Trisha Alexander. We're wondering if you'd be willing to tell us more about either of them."

"I cannot remember anything anymore. That was a long time ago."

"Sir, we're convinced that questionable and unethical deals were made here at this campus with the U.S. Army."

"Well, former President Nixon did it for a while in the White House."

Jennifer held up the old newspaper. "This Gazette article further states that before the charges were brought by the FBI and her arrest imminent, Dean Alexander committed suicide the following day."

Dr. Cummings seemingly became more agitated and said, "Before I tell you anymore, miss, I must warn you that there are individuals in high positions around here that will be extremely upset if they find out that you are going around asking these damn questions. I'm one of those people. Good day to both of you. Now let the past stay put.

Leave things as they are. Am I clear?"

The young couple nodded, turned, and walked away. They watched as the doctor entered a white stretched limo with black windows and departed.

"Do you believe that crock?" asked Kyle.

"He may be right, you know. Maybe we're nosing into someone's business, and it's none of ours."

"But why would he care so much? If that sort of shit happened over twenty some years ago, those people won't come back to haunt."

"No, but history can repeat itself."

"Yeah, like we're all of a sudden going to solve an unsolved mystery from that era?"

"Listen, Kyle. I love you very much. I want to do what's right. If a wrong was done back then and we find means to correct something, we should go for it."

"But, Jen, you heard his warning. He means business."

"I know. And we've just ruffled a feather."

"I . . . I don't know. Our love, careers, reputations, and our friends could all be put in jeopardy. Over what for God's sake?"

"Kyle! I know absolutely nothing about the true identity of my real parents other than the fact that they both attended Farnsworth College in the late 1960s and they and their friends were all hippie drug users."

"Jen, I wonder if the Howsers knew who your real parents actually were."

Jen began to sob. "Mr. Lancer and Ms. Alexander knew who they were . . . They had to."

During the ride home from church, Kyle tried to recall pieces from his own past. Fragments were all that he could remember.

December 1970

Sergeant John Paul Sheridan was on medical leave in Hawaii with other seasoned combat veterans. They had faced one difficult battle situation after another. He had become a good soldier and a fine leader. His rise in rank indicated his leadership abilities. Those men that served under him were proud to have him as their sergeant.

During his stay, JP met his former high school sweetheart, a Ms. Suzanne Hardesty. She was an attractive model and was participating in a beauty pageant there. He and his buddies were pleasantly surprised when Suzanne and her girlfriends agreed to a date with the soldiers following the pageant.

One romantic encounter led to another, and following a moonlit time on the deserted beach, Suzanne and JP made passionate love.

The next day, Sergeant Sheridan returned back to the jungles of Southeast Asia while Suzanne resumed her college studies back in the States. Her career as a model was short-lived as she soon discovered she was carrying his baby son.

"I sort of remember my mom mentioning that my daddy had attended Farnsworth College upon his return from Vietnam and that was after his brother's drug overdose."

"Maybe those files we recently located could help reconstruct answers that we each need to know."

"You're right, Jen. I believe both of our pasts are somewhere buried in those damn files."

"Do we look for answers there?" she sobbed.

"Well, it's the best lead we have."

"Why then does this old Dr. Cummings not want us to look?"

"The answer is obvious. He's done something that he's gotten away with all these years."

"Until now?"

"Hey, Jen, I don't recall seeing any barn near that stone house. Did you?"

"No, darling, no barn was visible to me."

"Let's see. If that took place in 1972, that's nearly twenty-two years ago. Maybe the barn was destroyed or torn down."

"That could be. We'll have to go back some time and look for evidence of it."

Following their Sunday brunch, Kyle and Jennifer returned to the Farnsworth campus. The sun reappeared following a brief shower and made the autumn foliage glisten. As they walked past the student union, they decided to attend the memorial service for Dean Henson in the college's chapel. They were joined by hundreds of Farnsworth's students and faculty members. The chapel filled quickly as two o'clock approached.

As they sat down toward the front of the church, they watched the solemn procession enter the rear of the church. Dean Henson's widow, the former Ms. Kiki Flaund who was now nearly fifty years old, came in carrying the urn containing her husband's ashes.

"That was quick," stated Kyle.

"What was, dear?"

"That they've already cremated him."

"It doesn't take long anymore," Jennifer stated affirmatively.

The college chaplain began the service, and the congregation stood and sang "Rock of Ages." After everyone was seated, newly appointed Dean Witherspoon walked slowly to the mike and began to speak. Suddenly, there was a commotion in the rear of the church.

"Would you get a load of that!" exclaimed Kyle.

"Yes!" stated Jennifer. "And who could be so rude? Especially at a time like this"

Everyone turned to look. A scuffle had erupted between an outsider and several of the ushers.

"The bastard got what he deserved!" his voice echoed through the hushed congregation. After a brief struggle, the intoxicated man was subdued and removed. The service quickly resumed.

"Did you hear that?" Jennifer asked while inconspicuously looking around.

"Everyone heard that! What a jerk!" chuckled Kyle.

"Please, everyone. I would like to resume," requested Dean Witherspoon. "May I have your attention once more? As many of you know, Dean Henson was very well liked by everyone here at Farnsworth College."

"Except the bastard that killed him," whispered Kyle.

"Under our dearly departed Dean Henson's leadership, the library project was completed, along with the addition of the new student housing units. This year's fundraiser received the highest pledged amount ever. Many of you literally grew up under his leadership and guidance during the past fourteen years. He spent countless hours, after becoming the dean, helping this college continue to heal its many wounds. He personally resolved all of his predecessor's mistakes."

"More like covered them up," whispered Kyle to Jennifer.

"Sush! Behave yourself."

"Dr. Joseph Henson was a graduate of this fine institute in 1972, received his master's degree in 1974 and his PhD in Law from the University of Maryland in 1979. Since becoming dean in 1980, he instilled a new sense of alliance to this institution by its staff and students. May we never forget his memory nor the legacy of commitment he left us and our beloved Farnsworth College. May God rest his soul."

The congregation rose and sang "Beyond the Sunset."

Following the service, Kyle and Jennifer stood in a nearby parking lot and commented on what the new dean had just said.

"I like his emphasis on 'all' his mistakes." Kyle smiled.

"No, stupid. Not his, but his predecessor's mistakes," scolded Jennifer. "Look over there. Professor Moore is leaving with Professor Hill and Dean Witherspoon."

"So what's that supposed to mean?"

"Mmmm, maybe they're best friends or simply just co-conspirators."

"Jen! I think you're seeing too damn much into this file-cabinet thing."

14

As Kyle and Jennifer drove out of the parking lot, they passed the political science department building. Kyle noticed several campus police cars quickly pulling up near the entrance. The campus police scurried into the building with weapons drawn like they were late for someone's surprise drug bust.

"Now why, on a Sunday afternoon, would they be running into that classroom building?"

"I don't rightfully know, darling. Again it's none of our business."

"Don't be so sure. Look!"

Shortly thereafter, they saw the campus police leading a man out of the building in handcuffs.

"That's the same person who yelled out during the dean's eulogy in the chapel."

"You're right," said Jennifer. "And I think I know him."

As the police cars departed with their passenger, Jennifer told Kyle, "Oh god! It's the dean's administrative assistant, Mr. Vognar."

"He said that Dean Henson had gotten what he deserved."

"Yes, Kyle. But no one deserves a knife in their chest like poor Dean Henson got."

"Kyle, go see if the building is locked."

"Why, Jen?"

"If it's open, let's go back to Professor Hill's office and get some more file folders please!"

"Jen! You must be kidding."

"No, Kyle. I'm not. I'm convinced those files contain very important information about our parents' lives."

"You're serious, aren't you?"

"Yes, let's go."

They approached the building and saw that the ground-level entrance was indeed unlocked. Upon entering the lower level, they walked down the silent corridor. Kyle unlocked Professor Hill's office door. As soon as they entered the back storage room, Kyle's eyes widened.

"Damn, just get a look at all this shit they've brought in here."

"I thought you told me you'd cleaned up in here."

"I did. The file cabinet is in that corner. Here, help me move these boxes."

They restacked the new storage boxes to a point where Kyle could again unlock and open the old cabinet.

"This top drawer contained files on staff members. They're pretty messed up."

"It appears that someone's already taken a lot of stuff out."

"The next drawer was labeled for Professor Hill's student papers from years ago. The lower drawers have the student files, and they're fairly intact."

"Well, we already have a file on Ms. Alexander. Who's left?"

Scanning the top file drawer, she exclaimed, "Here's files on Professor Henry Prestol and one on Dr. William Gray."

Stooping beneath her open file drawer, Kyle mentioned, "Prestol info was in Alexander's file that we looked at last night."

"You're quite right, Mr. Holmes."

"Okay, take these. See what student files you want."

"God! Check this out!"

"What, Kyle?"

"There are files here on practically every class member in the class of 1972!"

"Well, take any file that seems familiar to you."

Kyle anxiously scanned the folders and then selected several more files.

"Kyle, come on! Do you really think these files will tell us anything about our past?"

"Listen, if I can find out anything new about my daddy's past life, it will well definitely be worth the effort."

Clutching the file folders, she said, "Yes, I know. Maybe one of these characters knew something about our parents."

"I hope so, Jen. It'll mean a lot."

"Okay, Kyle. Let's go. It's getting late. I'll bring our treasures."

From a window in the administration building, Professor Hill watched Kyle and Jennifer leave the political science building carrying file folders. He smiled and reached for the phone. "Hello. This is Professor Roger Hill at Farnsworth College. Please advise Dr. Cummings that my little graduate assistant mouse has taken more of the bait."

The young couple drove home feeling happy to have secured some more files. At least they had a good start, and Kyle felt especially excited that he may have a file with information pertaining to his deceased daddy's college activities. As they drove along, they continued to ponder everything they had witnessed since that fateful past Thursday morning.

Later that Sunday afternoon, Kyle and Jen arrived back at their apartment from the college. Jen's curiosity about the true story of her parents' identity had been bothering her the past several days. As they entered into the tiny attic apartment, Jen told her boyfriend, "I have decided to call my aunt Florence. She should be home."

"Who's she?"

"My adoptive mom's sister. She's in her seventies."

"Sounds like another good lead."

Jen put down their file folders, entered the bedroom, and located her address book. After finding the number, she dialed and waited.

A weak little voice answered.

"Hello, Aunt Florence, Jennifer Howser here."

"Jennifer, dear! How are you doing in your graduate studies?"

"Just fine, I wanted to let you know that I'm engaged to Kyle Sheridan who attends here and is also a grad student."

"Well, let me give you my congratulations. Your parents, God rest their souls, would have been so proud of your successes."

"Yes, Aunt Florence. I suppose they would have. The other reason I called tonight was that Kyle and I are doing a genealogy project, and I really could use some help, you know, since I was adopted and you were very close to my adoptive parents."

"Darling Jennifer, the only information your adoptive mother ever gave me about your birth parents was that your real mother's name was Melanie and your supposedly father's name was Ricky."

"Oh my god! No. This can't be true!"

"What is it, dear?" asked Kyle who was standing in the kitchen with a look of concern.

"Aunt Florence! My fiancé's father had a brother twenty-four years ago named Ricky Sheridan, and his girlfriend was a Melanie Dulane. They are now both deceased."

"If they are the same Ricky and Melanie that my sister referred to, then your fiancé is really your first cousin! Oh, Jennifer . . . how could you!"

"But, Aunt Florence, I didn't know we were related! For God's sake . . . what should I do? We've had intercourse often, and I'm now pregnant!" Jennifer began to cry hysterically as Kyle quickly entered the bedroom.

"Calm down, dear. What's wrong?"

"It's . . . Aunt Florence."

Taking the receiver, Kyle became angrier. "Who the hell are you to make my Jen start crying?"

"And what gives you, young man, the right to make love to your first cousin?"

"What the hell are you talking about?"

"That's right, Mr. Kyle Sheridan," Aunt Florence sternly said.

"Your late uncle Ricky was Jennifer's real father! You figure it out. Goodbye."

Click.

"No! Jen! It's not true. We're not related . . . Are we?"

Through her sobbing, she nodded affirmative and turned away. He left the room and felt totally confused. He went and sat at the kitchen table, pondering the meaning of her statement. Soon, tears of frustration welled up, and he buried his face in his hands crying,

"How could this be happening?"

A short time later, the bedroom door opened, and Jen came and sat at the table with him saying, "Kyle, I love you so much. But it's wrong to be living and sleeping together if we're really that closely related."

"Stop talking that way," he argued back.

"Kyle, I'll move back to the dorm tomorrow until we can prove otherwise."

"Oh, Jen! I so want you to be my wife. How were we to know with our parents gone and surviving relatives not talking?"

"I know, Kyle," she cried. "I know." She moved closer, and they hugged each other tight.

He whispered in her ear, "Please stay with me. Leaving could be dangerous." They separated from the hug, and he told her, "No one knows if we are related, just that we're a loving couple. I think we should continue to work closely on this mystery, and who knows? Maybe the Ricky that your aunt mentioned wasn't my late uncle. There's lots of Rickys in this world."

After the young couple settled their nerves down, they turned their attention to more urgent problems of homework assignments and how to get their reports typed for Professor Moore's eight-o'clock class tomorrow morning.

When the reports were typed, it was time for bed. After turning out the lights in the apartment, Kyle, who was undressed down to his white Jockey briefs, began assisting Jen with her buttons and snaps.

He carefully undid each one. He gently kissed her exposed nipples and moved his hand downward, pulling her delicate lacy panties with them. She slowly slid his briefs down at the same time. She put her warm arms around his waist. She demonstrated again her ability to please her man in the way he loved the most. Soon the young lovers tumbled around in the bed kissing each other passionately before falling off to sleep.

15

Day Six
Monday
September 19, 1994

Monday morning, the alarm clock radio told them about a clear blue sky day, which lay ahead. After quick showers and breakfast, they left their apartment and drove to Farnsworth's campus.

"I think Professor Moore will be very pleased with our reports," smiled Jennifer.

"I hope so. We, I mean you, love, spent a lot of time on them."

"Are you going to work with Professor Hill today?"

"Yeah, and I'm going to spend some more quality time in the old file cabinet storage room."

"Just be discreet about it. We don't want to be accused on any wrongdoings."

After they left their apartment that morning, they drove by a parked, unmarked tan car with tinted windows. It was near the entrance of the parking lot. A man, dressed as Pennsylvania State Trooper, began conversing on his two-way radio. "The two suspects have left their apartment, Dr. Cummings."

Following their eight-o'clock class, Jennifer decided to spend some time in the new library. Kyle headed to the political science building. Seeing Professor Hill crossing the street, Kyle waved him down.

"Good morning, Professor Hill. Mind if I work a little while in your office?"

"Not at all, Mr. Sheridan, I'm going there now. Join me."

"Thanks," replied Kyle.

"That was a fitting tribute service for Dean Henson yesterday. Did you get to attend?"

"Yes, sir. My fiancée and I attended and thought it was nice."

"I still can't understand about Mr. Vognar."

"Isn't he the dean's secretary?" asked Kyle.

"The man was beside himself with apparent grief and must have gotten really drunk."

"Jen and I saw him getting handcuffed by campus police and taken away yesterday in front of this building."

"You did. Huh."

Kyle and the professor entered his office. Professor Hill closed the door and locked it. Suddenly, he barked out a command. "Have a seat, young Mr. Sheridan!"

"Sir, what fuck!?" Kyle asked as he quickly grabbed for a nearby chair.

"Old things are beginning to happen again. You know, like déjà vu. I must warn you and your girlfriend not to interfere."

"Professor Hill, I . . . I don't understand?"

"The man who murdered Dean Henson was named Teddy Lancer."

"Yes. It was on the TV news, and I read about it in the Gazette. What's that have to do with me?" pleaded Kyle.

"You were observed conversing twice with an elderly medical doctor named Travis Cummings. He was the former army officer who was in charge of a top secret project back in the early 1970s at Fort Douglas. This man is still extremely dangerous. He has a legion of devout, mindless, and fanatical followers at his disposal immediately if needed."

"I still don't understand, Professor."

"Son, for your own safety and that of your fiancée, don't say anything further to Dr. Cummings."

Kyle's head reeled. How was he observed talking to Dr. Cummings? He had not seen anyone who even looked suspicious nearby at those times.

"Ted Lancer was one of Cummings' hit squad goons. He had just been released from a state prison after serving twenty-two years for arson. He was supposed to have survived if that damn fire escape hadn't collapsed."

"Professor Hill, I never intended to meddle into others' affairs. Honest."

"I know, Mr. Sheridan. But by your girl asking Dr. Cummings about the late female dean, Ms. Alexander, both of you have opened up a real can of worms."

"Well, sir, I won't make that mistake again."

"If you do, you'll have sealed your fate! And I'm not joking."

Later, Kyle met Jennifer in the lower section of the campus library. She showed him some items on the microfiche machine. The rest of their afternoon was spent inside of the archives section finding and sorting bits and pieces of information. What they discovered was a literal treasure trove of information about student antiwar protest activities, changes in campus policies, and reported student drug overdoses all of which had been published by the local press. These articles dated between 1969 through 1974. Jennifer made notes of dates and featured campus activities.

Fort Douglas
U.S. Army Medical Research Facility, Maryland
December 1969

Farnsworth College's chemistry professor Henry Prestol and psychology professor William Gray were met by Henry's younger brother. He was an explosive weapons expert, First Lieutenant David Prestol, USA. He had recently returned from his first tour of duty in Vietnam, wearing a Bronze Star for combat valor. The youthful lieutenant and several other junior officers greeted and escorted their guests from the parking lot. Upon entering the building, they were greeted by Army MPs. They were heavily armed security and led the visitors to a small office in an underground bunker. They entered the room and saw a highly decorated army major. He wore both a Bronze and Gold Star along with a Purple Heart and was seated at a desk. Guards stood at the doorway and brought the men forward. Lieutenant David saluted and introduced the professors to the major.

"Professors, welcome to my lair. I'm Major Travis Cummings, MD, and I have a situation to deal with. You have been invited to participate in an historic top secret medical research project. It involves each of your talents and resources. You come here highly recommended and extremely qualified."

"Major, we're simple college professors with daily classes and limited money for secret military research work," commented Henry.

"Money will not be an issue, but your time is valuable. I completely understand."

"Excuse me, Major," asked Bill. "Why did you contact us?"

"Both of you are leaders in your fields. I've read your writings and viewed your portfolios. Quite impressive, gentlemen, if I must say so myself."

The major dismissed the guards and continued to go into more details about the proposed new research project. Both professors and the lieutenant seemed intrigued over the prospect of being involved in such an ambitious undertaking. The major's project involved using chemical formulas that Henry had recently discovered and held the patents to while teaching at Farnsworth College. Major Cummings wondered if, in theory, Henry's experiments would be able to be used in treating returning army veterans from Vietnam.

Many of our soldiers are suffering from the effects of the jungle defoliant Agent Orange. Bill, on the other hand, had extensive documented research experience with hallucinogenic drugs such as PCP and LSD. Sadly, many of his patients from his San Francisco's Height-Asbury District experiment during 1964–1968 had overdosed and died as a result. He explained that fact and for his personal well-being, he returned to the classroom. He began teaching at Farnsworth College last semester rather than remain in private practice.

"This research project has been classified under the code name of CAVE, which converted to your civilian terms means 'civilian and army voluntary experiences.' Lieutenant Prestol will be returning to Vietnam later this summer in another capacity. His new objective will involve recon missions that will also have significant impacts on this project. Oh, yes. He was also the person to recommend both of you. Think about it, Professors. I really could use your help with this one."

"We'll consider your most generous offer, Major Cummings," said Dr. William Gray.

"Major, there is one more thing," asked chemistry professor Henry Prestol.

"That is, Professor?"

"Sir, I'm very opposed to our government's involvement in this undeclared war. I am, fortunately, over the age for the draft. My students know and understand my antiwar position. Many of my students are beginning to show signs of unrest over this unfair conflict. I personally don't see much support from my students for such research if the military is connected to it."

"I completely understand, Professor Prestol. Their logic many have to be changed to convince them that this research would benefit them also."

"In other words, Major," interjected Professor Gray, "the allure of free hallucinogenic drugs might do the trick."

"Nothing can begin without your help," said the major. "Gentlemen, it's been a pleasure meeting both of you. I sincerely hope we all can work together for healthier veterans."

Lieutenant David saluted the major. All the men exchanged handshakes and left the major's bunker for the officer's club. Following dinner, the lieutenant's guests, Henry and Bill, were driven back to Farnsworth College.

"It's a lot to think about," Bill told his colleague. "Does the major have any realistic vision of how this research could really play out?"

"I see his point for helping the returning veterans," commented Henry.

"It could take hundreds of lab animals to test my formulas, considering the thought of eventually getting human guinea pigs for our research hasn't been done since the A-bomb tests from the early 1950s."

The two brilliant professors discussed Major Travis Cumming's proposal late into the night. After Bill had left to go home, Henry's phone rang before midnight. It was his brother.

"Hey, brother, I'm glad you finally got to meet the major."

"David, I must give you credit. I know we've had our differences in the past. I didn't support you entering the army at first. But you have made me feel very proud of your accomplishments."

"Henry, I've loved you as a brother and always looked up to you while growing up. I remember how you teased me with that chemistry set you bought. Our parents were furious when you demonstrated how to blow up the outhouse!" Both men laughed. "The major is on a mission. I believe he would like to retire from the army a very wealthy man."

"Maybe he believes through us he can," commented Henry.

"Perhaps we all could benefit from this CAVE project. Other covert military missions have made many individuals quite wealthy in their old age."

"I suppose you're right, David. We all could benefit if we have a mission.

Please continue, my little brother."

"If you and Dr. Gray use the major's research money and begin your own pharmaceutical production of hallucinogenic products. You could hire some of your students as distributors among the six local college campuses. And in addition to that source allow me to contribute from the major's covert ops. We could amass a fucking fortune."

"Would the major allow us to do that?"

"Once he's included in the decision making. Besides, he's powerful, influential, and quite thorough."

"Things must be done above board at all times," insisted Henry.

"Get Dr. Gray to do the documentation. Let him keep secret files on all the participants, both military and civilian."

"Allow me to sleep on this one."

"Good night, my brother. Sleep well."

Once Henry hung up the phone to retire for the night, David left his quarters to meet with Major Cummings in his underground bunker.

"I believe, sir, that my brother and his colleague with accept your offer."

"If and when that's the case, you will become a key player."

"I appreciate that, Sir.

Farnsworth College Dean's Office
December 1969
The Next Day

Professors William Gray and Henry Prestol sat in front of Dean Hayward's desk.

"Bill and I met yesterday with army Major Travis Cummings, MD, at Fort Douglas. We were invited to participate in a new medical research project for returning sick veterans. They apparently are being exposed to some poisonous or toxic substances during jungle warfare. The Army Medical Facility at Fort Douglas will be the treatment center for these soldiers. The major would like to invite our campus into a joint venture with full government funding."

"What specifically do they need from us?" asked the dean.

"Henry's latest patents are quite high on their interests," replied Bill.

"Bill's prior research from his San Francisco experiments was also discussed," added Henry.

"What benefits would there be for Farnsworth College?"

"Honestly, Earl," said Henry, "this could bring us millions in research grants and make our college's name quite well-known."

"I know for a fact that my psychology department would be the bases for continuing studies for future generations of Farnsworth's scholars. Even on the graduate level."

"That's something I could not see happening for years with our current status," lamented Dean Hayward.

The men continued to discuss the advantages of the Colonel's CAVE project and were convincing enough to get Earl's permission to accept. Once again, the three men toasted Champagne to the success of Farnsworth's joint venture.

16

Kyle, carrying several file folders in his knapsack, met Jen, and together they left the library building for home. It was shortly before 5:00 p.m. Following dinner and a brief roust in the bedroom, Kyle and Jennifer turned their attention to several new file folders that he had obtained earlier this morning and smuggled home. Jennifer felt a strange sensation overcome her as she lifted a particular folder.

"Kyle, take a look at this one."

"Who's it belong to?" he asked.

"The name is Richard Sheridan, Jr.!"

"God, Jen! That's my dead uncle's file! May I take a look?"

"Be my guest. His file's quite thick."

"I didn't realize until now he was involved with all this stuff. I'll bet my bottom dollar, my grandparents don't know shit about any of this."

With a frown and a deep voice, she said in a mockingly way, "From the size of this file, it looks to me like he was very deep in it!"

"Okay, now. Be nice."

Kyle began to read one of the recorded reports.

File Eight
Fort Lauderdale, Florida
March 1971

One evening during the spring break, Ricky Sheridan, Jr., the twenty-one-year-old junior classman at Farnsworth College, and chemistry professor Henry Prestol were seated poolside at a luxurious oceanfront hotel. Joining them at their table were two older Latin American men named Alfonso and Juan. As the men talked, Professor Prestol proudly said, "Gentlemen, I service nearly five thousand college clients on six regional campuses." The professor stood up, raised his cocktail glass, and proclaimed, "Mr. Sheridan, my All-American junior at Farnsworth College, has, as my distributor, helped me move into the position of a major drug supplier for these campuses."

The men applauded his efforts. Ricky and Professor Prestol shook hands with their guests. The professor told them, "Thank you. We couldn't have done it without your help."

Alfonso said, "We'll see that His Excellency is informed of your success, Professor Prestol. We'll personally see to it that only the purest coke and heroin is sent to your lab for your research project."

Professor Henry Prestol replied, "Tell His Excellency that the American students are responding to my new drug, Sernyl, better than expected."

"We're pleased about that, Professor. May I inquire as to your account status?" asked Juan.

"Every month my brother, army lieutenant David Prestol, currently stationed in Vietnam, and I make large amounts of cash to our Mercantile account. Thank you, gentlemen. Good night."

As the Latino men walked away, Professor Prestol lit a cigarette and said,

"Come, Mr. Richard Sheridan, Jr., the young ladies are waiting to celebrate your twenty-first birthday."

They left the poolside and entered the brightly lit hotel lobby. Jennifer told Kyle, "See, that stationary from the metal box tells us that there could be a fortune in the Harrisburg Mercantile Bank, and we might have the lockbox numbers!"

"We'll find out tomorrow if there actually is such an account. And I remember growing up, hearing stories from my grandparents about Uncle Ricky being a real dissent student with the antiwar movement but never a word about his apparent drug connections."

"And yet your daddy, JP, Ricky's younger brother, served in Vietnam while all of this was going down?" asked Jen.

"Yes, ain't that some more shit!" he replied almost with a laugh.

"Ricky was the great All-American jock, and apparently could ever do nothing wrong. He got a fucking deferment for college, but my daddy, who was more the artistic type, got drafted. Guess he didn't have the grades."

"Or the right connections," she replied. "This old newspaper clipping shows a picture of your uncle Ricky with his girlfriend, a Ms. Melanie Dulane."

Jennifer pondered if she really was looking at a photo of her birthparents. She seemed very surprised at her next find from the file. "And here's a letter from Vietnam that looks like some sort of love letter from a JP Sheridan to Ms. Melanie!"

"Oh no!" cried Kyle. "This can't be true! My daddy dated that bitch too!"

"What the hell!" she replied in shock. "How awful!" "Now we've got a serious problem."

"Kyle. Please tell me what kind of problem."

"Jen, my daddy finally married my birthmother, Suzanne Hardesty, in Washington, D.C., in 1973. I was nearly three years old by then and was living with her."

File Nine
Fort Douglas, Maryland
December 1971

Sergeant John Paul Sheridan had returned home from Vietnam last month to bury his year-older brother. Ricky's death had been ruled a suicide from a drug overdose. His girlfriend, Melanie, stood accused of his death. JP had spent the last thirty days with his bereaved parents who claimed that the army was somehow connected with Ricky's death.

JP had been introduced to Colonel Travis Cummings, MD, in Vietnam earlier on. Upon his arrival Stateside, the colonel arranged for JP to be reassigned to Fort Douglas, which was close to Farnsworth College. The colonel also introduced him as Ricky's successor in assisting Professor Henry Prestol with CAVE operations.

JP had served proudly under Henry's brother, Lieutenant David Prestol, and finally made the connection about how the two brothers had established a working relationship. They used money from Vietnam and the colonel's unending government grants to fund their own drug research and distribution.

JP had no idea how involved Ricky had become, and after witnessing so-called student volunteers being totally mind-conditioned from Professor Prestol and the colonel's research, they knew how much he knew of their operation.

Upon his arrival at Fort Douglas, the new sergeant was immediately injected, rendered unconscious, his uniform removed by a team of technicians, and strapped to a gurney. Once the gurney was wheeled into the secret research facility, the reconditioning process began.

Fort Douglas Army Research Lab
December 1971

Young JP Sheridan sat in the outer office as Colonel Cummings finished his staff briefing. Hearing voices in argumentative tones behind the door, he began feeling more uncomfortable as the minutes ticked by. The heated discussion suddenly stopped, and the office door opened.

"Sergeant Sheridan! Get your ass inside this instant," ordered the colonel.

He stood up, straightened his uniform, and took a deep breath. As he entered the office, he stopped and saluted.

"At ease, Sergeant," said Colonel Cummings as he returned JP's salute.

"This is Professor William Gray, head of psychology, and Professor Henry Prestol, head of chemistry, from Farnsworth College."

JP extended his hand and was warmly greeted by the men. "I served with your late brother, David."

"Yes," replied the professor. "David had entrusted you with much responsibility concerning his search and recovery operations."

"Professor Prestol, Lieutenant David was a great platoon leader and a dedicated individual. You know, a man on a mission."

"Yes, Sergeant. He will be missed by a lot of people. He was a crucial link in my own operation. The colonel here tells me you are planning to remain for the trial of the Dulane girl. It's really sad that we each have lost our brothers."

Dr. Gray said, "Both of you men have lost a great deal. Losing both Ricky Sheridan and Lieutenant David Prestol has been a real setback to our operations both here and in Vietnam. Sergeant Sheridan, the professor and I have a proposal to make. The colonel assures us that you are the right man for the job."

JP eyed the three men with suspicion and said, "I know about David recovering stolen art objects and collecting the reward money, but I really have no clue as to what my hippie brother was doing here at Farnsworth College."

Henry took a few puffs on his cigar as Bill Gray looked intensely at JP. "Your brother was our distributor at Farnsworth campus and six other regional colleges."

He appeared puzzled. "Distributor of what?" he asked.

"Sernyl," said the colonel. "It's a powerfully addictive hallucinogenic reformulated and manufactured by Professor Prestol here at Farnsworth College and also at this Army medical facility."

"You're saying that my late brother Ricky was a drug dealer?"

"The best," insisted Henry. "He knew every important college contact connector."

Dr. Gray said, "Ricky got us top dollars for the stuff."

"As you can see, Sergeant," replied the colonel, "the course is already laid out before you. All you need to do is to become our new jockey."

JP thought he had never heard of anything so preposterous before. But then things began to make more sense, and he said with a broad smile, "What's in it for me?"

Henry laid his cigar on the corner of the colonel's desk and said, "Your brother's cut was nearly one-quarter of a million in less than one year."

"Shit! That's major money. My buddies earn a dollar and a quarter per hour flipping hamburgers." Laughed JP.

"Well, Sergeant. Can we count on you to follow in your brother's footsteps?" asked Dr. Gray.

"If I agree to work with you, I want one-fourth of the future profits, and I want Ricky's share transferred to my bank account as a signing-on bonus."

The three men nodded their approval, and everyone shook hands in agreement.

"Sergeant, there may not be much money left from Ricky's account since he was so addicted to the stuff and required a constant supply."

"So Ricky was a junkie too?"

"Both he and the Dulane girl went through a fortune on their drug habits."

"My god!" lamented JP. Suddenly he became overcome with emotion.

"You! You bastards! You did this to my brother Ricky and his girlfriend. You never cared about them. Just how much money Ricky would make you!" he cried. "And you want me to do the same thing!"

Dr. Gray moved in behind JP as he leaned over the colonel's desk. With approving eyes, Dr. Gray quickly injected him with a hypodermic syringe. JP then collapsed on the floor.

Colonel Cummings reached over and pressed his intercom button. "Bring a gurney to my office. We have a new volunteer."

"Yes, Colonel. Right away."

17

Several hours later, JP's body shook violently on the gurney that held him prisoner. The young sergeant drifted in and out of consciousness. He had no idea how long he had been in this room once he regained his composure. He felt sheer panic as he realized he was naked under a hospital gown, and his arms and legs were restrained along with being blindfolded and having a bite gag in his mouth. Suddenly, he drifted off, and his mind ran wild with hallucinogenic visions. Bright colors erupted in a kaleidoscope before his closed eyes, and he continued hearing voices from unseen sources.

Behind a two-way wall mirror stood the colonel and Dr. Gray. "How soon will he be ready to begin?" asked the colonel as they watched a military orderly attach a replacement bottle to his intravenous feeding tube.

"He's just received the second IV, Colonel. The whole process takes twenty-four hours. He'll be ready by morning."

"Excellent," replied the colonel. "Professor Prestol is anxious for his new volunteer assistant to begin the distributions."

"Sergeant Sheridan's conditioning program has an extra bonus feature."

"Really, Dr. Gray? What is it?"

"Do you remember how young Ricky Sheridan would often question some of our commands because he realized that they went against his ethical beliefs from his childhood upbringing?"

"Yes, I particularly recall him damn near botching up a mission to firebomb that draft office in Ambersburg last year. Something was said about the risk of being caught and arrested by the local jurisdiction. That was a very close call."

"Professor Prestol made an adjustment to the formula that inhibits a reactionary response to potential dangerous assignments. This should allow our Sergeant Sheridan to follow your instructions to the tee without questioning your motives."

"Sounds like that is what we've been so anxious to accomplish with this whole damn program. Remind me to congratulate him the next time we meet."

"Dean Alexander will also be pleased to learn that her interests will now be protected by her sergeant lying here."

JP continued to struggle against his bonds and cried out for relief from his torment and those who were subjecting him to this horrific treatment. Little could he realize what potential he would possess to carry out the will of the colonel to further his sick agenda.

The following morning, he was fitted with a different mouth gag that kept his jaw pried open, and remained blindfolded. He was then removed from the gurney and placed into a wheelchair. The orderly secured him tightly to the chair before taking him to another part of the medical research facility. There he was reattached to a wooden chair, which was bolted to the floor in the center of a laboratory room. JP's head reeled, and he was covered with perspiration from being deprived of his voice, sight, and movement.

Army orderlies scurried about attaching electrodes to numerous parts of his nude body. He thought that he heard light switches being either being turned off or on but was unable to tell.

New sensations began happening throughout his entire being. Every nerve ending felt like it was being stimulated. Suddenly he realized that low voltage electrical currents were being passed through various parts of him. Briefly and not causing too much discomfort at first, these charges became slightly more sensational as he realized someone must be controlling the voltage regulator.

Again, a new sensation of panic overwhelmed him as he realized who was controlling the current.

"Welcome to my specially appointed adjustment center," said Colonel Cummings. Then continuing, he said, "You're most promising accomplishments lie ahead of you."

JP struggled to respond to his captor.

"Oh, don't waste your strength here. Just relax a bit. We won't be long, so then you'll be ready to take on the world."

He didn't have a clue to what the colonel was referring to but soon felt a charge of electricity that penetrated his very being. His mind felt as if he was being suspended above his own body looking down! Had he died and his soul was being torn away from his body? He had never experienced a drug-induced trip like this ever.

Darkness surrounded him, and he embraced it like a lover. After he was released from the wooden chair, he was again placed on a gurney for a final journey. This trip led to an elevator that carried the sergeant and his handlers to another level of the facility. His blindfold and gag were removed, and he was dressed in a specially designed military uniform. For the first time, JP confronted his tormentors.

"Welcome back, Sergeant Sheridan. How are you feeling?" Dr. Gray asked.

"That was one hell of a trip, sir. I feel all right, but something feels very different."

"Come, look at yourself."

JP dizzily steadied himself and glanced into a nearby mirror. "My god! What's happened?"

"You are not the same person you were when you arrived."

His hands shook as he felt his face. His hair had become white, and he looked much older.

"This is a normal physical reaction to the drugs that you ingested. Over time, your body will adjust, and your appearance should return to your post-treatment look," replied Dr. Gray in a reassuring tone. "It's all right," he said to the attendants. "You may leave."

Following the orderlies' departure, Dr. Gray addressed JP. "You have a new life and a new mission."

"Sir, what do you mean?"

"Your late brother, Ricky, and most of his friends entered into this treatment program and were transformed into mindless robots who blindly obeyed the colonel's and Professor Prestol's orders."

"But I don't understand why, and what's this have to do with me?"

"Up to now, individuals who participated in the treatment program just followed orders. They did the colonel's dirty work and made money for both the colonel and Professor Prestol. But then something went wrong last month, and Ricky had to be terminated."

"You mean his death was planned?"

"Both your brother and Lieutenant David Prestol's death were staged by the colonel for basically double crossing him."

"How awful! I had no idea," lamented JP.

Suddenly, the door was pushed opened and an armed security guard yelled, "Attention on deck!"

He immediately turned and faced the door and saluted.

"At ease, soldier," replied Colonel Cummings, returning JP's salute. "How is our patient, Dr. Gray?"

"He's ready to serve under your command, sir."

"Excellent. Sergeant John Paul Sheridan, I've decorated you once before in Vietnam. Now, as a new member of my elite special armed guard, you will follow me to the briefing room for your first assignment."

"Thank you, Colonel," he said proudly while saluting.

JP said nothing further to Dr. Gray as he left the room. The colonel gave the thumbs-up to Farnsworth's psychology professor Dr. Gray as he also began to leave.

File Ten
Gettysburg, Pennsylvania
January 1972

Mary and Richard Sheridan, Sr., sat in silence as their surviving son, army sergeant JP Sheridan, tried to explain the circumstances surrounding the overdose death of their oldest son, Ricky, Jr.

"Pop, Melanie and Ricky were users of a newly developed drug called Sernyl," he told them. "This drug changes their thinking patterns and makes the user more and more dependent."

"I remember Ricky complaining of poor vision and headaches," said his father.

"And the last time we talked to him on the phone, I could barely understand his talking, you know. He slurred his words. He had never done that before," lamented his mom.

"They were dead giveaways to his drug use," said JP.

"Oh, damn that girl!" cried Mary. "I knew, from the first time I met Melanie back in high school, she was bad for our dear Ricky."

"Where the hell did they get this drug from?" asked Richard.

"It's a long story that involves many people at Farnsworth College and the Army Research Lab at Fort Douglas."

"I should have known those Army Bastards were in on this."

"Pop, I believe that Ricky and Melanie actually volunteered to work for the Army as human guinea pigs."

"What the Hell!" Richard yelled. "No son of mine would do such a stupid-ass thing!"

"I'm sorry, Pop!" JP lamented. "That's what I've been able to find out since I got back from Vietnam to attend his funeral," he continued saying.

"And from the looks of things, the Army will deny any knowledge about its secret medical research involving student volunteers."

"Those bastards!" cried his father. "They've probably written off Ricky's life as an experiment that went wrong."

"Yeah," JP replied, shrugging his shoulders. "It seems that's what happened."

"Son," asked his Mom. "What are you going to do now?"

"It'll take the Army about two months to get all my records and stuff sent home so I can get discharged. Colonel Cummings has given me a temporary assignment in the intelligence unit. I'll continue to room and board at our Government's expense at Fort Douglas until my discharge."

"Well, son. All I have to say is be very careful. Those people are very sneaky. Your pop and I don't trust any of them."

"I completely understand and appreciate your concern. I'll be fine and I'll see you at Melanie's trial."

Richard stood up to see his son to the door and said, "I hope they throw the book at that hippie bitch. She'll never amount to nothing. She's a real burned-out loser. Wait till you see her."

"What about her baby?"

"That baby's no kin of mine. Ricky would have told us if he was the real father. Since he didn't, I'm sure that whore slept with half the fellows on Farnsworth's campus."

JP shrugged his shoulders again and said, "Suppose you're right, Pop."

"Damn straight! I'm right on this one."

Mary joined her husband at the door and said, "Goodbye son. Take care of yourself."

"Thanks. Love you both."

JP buttoned his jacket and opened the Army car that was waiting on him.

"Where to, Sergeant Sheridan?" asked the driver.

"I need to find Farnsworth's chemistry professor Dr. Henry Prestol. He's got a new shipment for me to distribute tomorrow."

"We'll be there in about twenty minutes."

"Fine!"

18

Tuesday afternoon was bright and sunny, and autumn colors were just beginning to show around Farnsworth's campus. Kyle left his design class as soon as the bell rang and headed down several flights of steps. Leaving Michaelson Hall, he joined Jennifer on a bench in the quad area.

"I've just spent over two solid hours on that damn microfiche machine and can't find any mention of this operation named CAVE in any of those old newspaper articles," replied Jen.

"Well, it probably wasn't general knowledge, especially if the army was involved."

"I did find the names of twelve students who committed suicide or overdosed on drugs during the years of 1970–74. That included your uncle Ricky in November 1972."

"Don't you see, Jen! Anyone who worked for chemistry professor Henry Prestol and army doctor Cummings was probably programmed to kill themselves if they weren't needed or tried to warn others about their bad experiences. Their deaths were probably made to look like suicides."

"Oh, Kyle. That's dreadful."

"And what was worse is that all those other so-called campus radicals were handled the same fucking way."

At the same time they were talking, they were being watched by security personnel from the roof of the political science building and listened to on a previously planted listening device that was concealed under the benches around the quad area. One was very near to where Kyle was seated. After watching through binoculars and listening on a headset, the guard relayed the developments over his walkie-talkie set.

"Sir, Max here. They're on a bench in the quad. The Sheridan boy is extremely agitated. The girl said she could not find any researched material about Operation CAVE in the library's archives."

"Very well, Sergeant. Keep me updated. Have them followed closely."

"Yes, Dr. Cummings. The team will not let them out of sight while there here on campus."

"I want them followed beyond this campus. I cannot afford to lose that boy. He's worth a fucking fortune. Is that understood?"

"Yes, sir. You can depend on your team, sir."

"I know. I made you that way. Over and out."

Later, inside their apartment, Kyle and Jennifer began to organize the sequence of events that led to the apparent suicide of Dean Alexander and the mysterious disappearance of chemistry professor Henry Prestol in 1972.

Saigon, South Vietnam
May 1971

Captain David Prestol entered the steamy and smoke-filled brothel hoping to meet Li. She had a reputation for being one of the best whores in Saigon.

He met her about two months earlier. Their time together was totally relaxing and perhaps the most sexually gratifying he had ever experienced.

She was truly a professional and commanded the highest prices.

Having recently returned from Cambodia with more recovered art objects, he proudly displayed his bankroll to the mistress at the door. She quickly escorted him upstairs to a room he had never seen before. The dimly lighted room had walls and drapes that were made of silk.

There was a circular bed with lots of satin pillows. Several mirrors were strategically placed for the clients to have the best views. There was also a mirror on the ceiling above the bed. Incense burned and soft music played.

He sat in his boxers on the bed playing with his dog tags and looking nervously around the brothel. Soon, he saw curtains move, and he heard a small giggle. When the curtains opened, Li stepped out wearing a sheer negligee. She slowly approached him as he stood up to greet her. After a lingering embrace, she removed her clothes and slid under the satin sheets, saying, "Oh, my American captain David Prestol. I so do want to love you and please you."

He quickly removed his boxers and climbed naked into the bed with her.

"Honey, you're just what this soldier needs tonight."

They embraced, and he allowed himself to become a slave to his own sexual emotions. She felt and smelled wonderful. They kissed, and he rolled over and let her hands begin to gently massage his naked back. She tenderly applied soothing oil and slowly seduced him into a hypnotic state.

As he closed his eyes under her spell, he failed to see her reflection in the mirror as she reached under the bed and pulled out a long-bladed knife. With several quick vicious stabs to his back, David's life flowed out of his wounded body.

Pulling a sheet around her, she emptied David's wallet of cash and ran laughing from the room.

Farnsworth College's Chemistry Department
May 1971

Ricky Sheridan, now a junior, entered the lab following lunch at the student union. He saw Professor Henry Prestol talking with two army officers whom he didn't recognize. When the soldiers left, Ricky approached the professor who was standing and staring out of the window.

"Excuse me, Professor Prestol. Who were those men?"

"They just notified me of my brother David's death in Saigon."

"Oh, Professor! I'm so sorry to hear that. I know how close you were to him."

Henry sat down and began speaking softly. "He had everything in the world going right for him, and he threw it all away on some goddamn prostitute!"

"Wasn't Captain Prestol killed in battle?"

"No, son. He was knifed by a girl in a Saigon whorehouse."

Ricky pulled up a nearby chair and sat down next to Henry who was gazing out of the lab window. He compassionately put his hand on Henry's shoulder and said, "Man! Now that's a heavy trip."

"Yes, and what a damn total waste of a good person!"

"Sir, I just received another letter from my brother JP in Vietnam."

"Yes. David wrote me quite a lot about your brother's outstanding performance in his platoon. In fact, your brother saved David's life when they were ambushed in the field."

"My brother received the Purple Heart and the Silver Star for that deed."

"Ricky, do me a favor."

"Sure, Professor Prestol, anything you need."

"Write to your brother JP and tell him that if he continues David's work, I'll see that Colonel Cummings gets him transferred to Fort Douglas after his tour is up."

"Sir, that would be terrific! He could even enroll here and work with us."

"We'll see. Goodbye, Ricky. I'll talk to you later."

"Fine, Professor. Sorry again about your brother's passing."

FBI Headquarters
Washington, D.C.
June 12, 1972

Psychology professor Dr. William Gray, who was recently fired from Farnsworth College, walked across Pennsylvania Avenue and entered the FBI building. He passed a security checkpoint and was directed to the elevators.

When he left the elevator, several agents greeted him and led him to the assistant director's office.

They entered a dimly lit room with the window shades drawn and were seated in high-back leather chairs around a large oval wooden conference table.

"Dr. Gray, I'm sorry Mr. Hoover couldn't be with us today because of his illness. I'm certain he would have been extremely interested in what you're about to tell us," said the assistant director. He then addressed the assembled group. "Gentlemen, what we have here is an extremely sensitive issue. Tell them, Dr. Gray."

"Certainly. Good morning, gentlemen. Thank you for taking time with me today. The army at Fort Douglas has been doing extensive medical research over the past two and a half years. The research team, since its conception, has been under the direction of army colonel Travis Cummings, MD. His assignment was supposedly to develop a new drug to counter the effects of the chemical Agent Orange. Several other teams in other states are doing similar research. It seems that many GIs were exposed to this toxic agent in Vietnam. However, in this particular research project, Dr. Cummings, with the assistance of chemistry professor Dr. Henry Prestol from nearby Farnsworth College, began using LSD, PCP, and the new formula of the drug Sernyl on human subjects."

"Dr. Gray, what was your involvement in this research project and when did you personally become aware of this new direction?"

"I was an original team member until last week when I was abruptly dismissed. The mind-altering experiments began last summer."

"And what exactly were your duties?"

"I was in charge of personally recruiting student volunteers from Farnsworth College to assist the army with their research. Each student had to get signed permission from Dean Alexander to come to me for drug counseling. I then contacted Colonel Cummings and informed him that I was recommending them for his treatment program."

"Did you realize that these young men and women were being used as human guinea pigs?" asked a senior agent.

"No, sir. I only knew that when a student finished this drug rehab program. Their thinking processes had been definitely altered significantly, and most could not participate normally within the college community. They also suffered from severe bouts of depression."

"What became of those students?" asked the assistant director.

"Many committed suicide by overdosing. Other healthy young males were reconditioned to become an elite group of a military-style campus police to protect the colonel's research project and Farnsworth's campus."

The assistant director told Dr. Gray, "Good God! If what you say is true, we'll have a real battle on our hands if we're to put a stop to all of this."

An older agent, who was a senior assistant to the director, spoke up, "Sir, I suggest that you inform Dean Alexander of our intentions to launch a full-scale FBI investigation into the corruption within Farnsworth's administration because of the recent rash of student suicides."

Fort Douglas Army Research Lab
June 13, 1972

Colonel Cummings approached Professor Henry Prestol who was seated looking through a microscope. The colonel put his hand on the professor's shoulder.

"Dr. Prestol, your new drug Sernyl is such an improvement. The subject's response is just what I had hoped for. You're truly a brilliant chemist."

He looked up while adjusting his glasses and asked, "What do you want, Colonel?"

Dr. Cummings leaned over and whispered in his ear, "I want your formula and a cut of your bank account."

Dr. Prestol turned his stool around and faced the colonel, saying, "The formula now belongs to the army. Remember you've already paid me enough for it. And who put that silly notion into your head that there's a secret bank account?"

"Let's say I simply overheard your late brother, David, tell his hospital room partner, a certain army sergeant named JP Sheridan, all about your elaborate plans. And that there's a fucking fortune that you've amassed of which I now want my share of it!"

"That must have been over two years ago. Nothing ever became of it."

"You're lying!" yelled Dr. Cummings, slamming his fists on the desk.

"Between you soaking up all of my hard-earned research dollars and acting as the drug kingpin for Farnsworth College and your late brother selling gems and stolen gold Buddha statues back to the Saigon government, I'd say you brothers have massed quiet a hefty sum."

"I'm afraid, Colonel, you've gotten the wrong picture."

"Bullshit! I'm putting you on notice, Dr. Prestol. I will find a way to get my share if I have to go to extremes to get it."

Professor Prestol flashed the irritated army doctor a broad smile. "Well, Colonel. I'd say you've gotten a damn good start."

"Go to hell, Professor."

Dr. Prestol began to laugh while replying, "Wait till Dean Alexander hears of this."

Acting frustrated, the colonel barked back, "She already has! Ha."

Tonight, inside Kyle and Jen's tiny apartment, the air was filled with much apprehension and unanswered questions. Jen told her lover, "This sheet is the minutes of a facility meeting where the dean, Ms. Alexander, fired psychology professor W. Gray."

"Gee, I wonder what he had done to piss her off," asked Kyle.

"According to these minutes, he had threatened to blackmail her with evidence he had obtained about another secret deal she had recently made with the U.S. Army at Fort Douglas."

"Was she a double agent for the Russians too?"

"I hardly think so. I think she was under enormous pressures as the first female dean to demonstrate her true leadership abilities."

"So she suspected everyone who didn't follow her game plan?"

"It certainly looks that way from this paper."

"The newspaper articles I found earlier today in the library were from the end of June 1972, and said that once the FBI investigation of Farnsworth began on the fifteenth, some unusual things began to happen."

"Really, like what?" inquired her boyfriend.

Near Farnsworth College Campus
June 15, 1972

That evening at dusk, Ms. Tricia Alexander, dean of Farnsworth College, carried a rope and climbed up a ladder onto the loft area of the wooden barn on her property. The old barn dated back to the early 1800s and was located behind her old stone farmhouse.

A single kerosene lantern burned nearby. She tied one end of the rope to a wood beam. She put the other end around her neck. She picked up and held the lantern as she jumped off from the high loft. The lantern fell from her grasp and ignited straw beneath her dangling feet.

Within a short time, the barn was completely engulfed in flames.

"Dean Alexander's suicide on her farm," said Jen, "and the sudden mysterious disappearance of Professor Henry Prestol must have occurred nearly at the same time."

"How convenient it was for the colonel. I wonder if Dr. Cummings got what he wanted. Did the FBI continue their investigation further?"

"Not for long. Two days later, the world's attention was refocused on the Watergate break-in on June 17. President Nixon's cronies became more important than some internal problems here at Farnsworth College."

Kyle began to laugh. "Wouldn't it be wild if, in fact, we could somehow prove that Colonel Travis Cummings's research subjects included former attorney general John Mitchell along with President Nixon's aids, John Ehrlichman, H. R. Haldeman, White House counsel John Dean, and even the Watergate burglars, Gordon Liddy, Howard Hunt, and James McCord!"

"Who knows, our late former president Nixon himself might have even been programmed."

"Well, Jen, I know I'm programmed for bed. Come join me. Plots and damn conspiracies always look better in the morning."

"Yes, Mr. Sheridan. The defense will rest."

19

Kyle's childhood memories continued to remain very fragmented. Before falling to sleep, he told Jen, "I remember when I was five years old, a young woman named Melanie came to visit my mom and daddy for what I thought was the first time."

Suzanne Sheridan's Home in Rose Hill Manor
May 2, 1976

Suzanne stood patiently and looked out of the second-floor window.

Her husband, John, had called earlier and informed her that his train had been delayed. The rain, which had started earlier this morning, continued throughout the day. The raindrops hitting the window sash sounded like applause. Suzanne closed her eyes and imagined she again was walking down the runway after winning another beauty pageant title.

She awoke from her daydream and glanced out the window, noticing a lone figure of a woman carrying a multicolored umbrella approaching her front door.

"Now who could that be?" Suzanne wondered.

The door chimes announced the unknown visitor. With her curiosity aroused, she quickly descended the stairs and unlocked the front door, allowing it to open on to the security chain.

"Yes, may I help you?"

The young woman appeared in the doorway and said, "Hello. My name is Melanie Dulane. I have been searching for some time to locate a John P. Sheridan. Does he live here?"

"Yes. He's my husband."

"Oh. I'm so glad to have found the right place. Is he home now?"

"I'm sorry, he's not. And I really don't know when he'll be back since his train has been delayed."

"Oh, I see."

"Is there a message I could give him for you?"

"Well, it's a complicated story, and he'd probably like to hear it in its entirety."

Noticing that Melanie seemed pale and hungry looking, Suzanne boldly invited her inside. "Would you like me to fix you a cup of tea and some cookies?"

"That would be delightful. I've been walking in this rain all day, and a dry place to sit would be fine. That is, if it's no trouble."

"I suppose not. My little boy should be getting off the school bus shortly, and he'll want a snack anyway. Come, Melanie. Join me."

"Thank you, Mrs. Sheridan. You're most kind."

"Please, you may call me Suzanne."

Entering the wide foyer, Melanie immediately focused on the recent family portrait hanging on the wall. "My, how JP's changed."

"You know John's nickname?"

"Yes. We go back to high school."

"Really! Then he'll be surprised to see you."

Melanie followed Suzanne into the kitchen and sat on a stool at the counter. As the water began to boil, a familiar sound echoed from the foyer.

"Mommy! I'm home!"

Five-year-old Kyle entered the kitchen, wearing a dripping yellow raincoat and hood. He also carried a soggy knapsack. "Who's she?"

"Son, this is Ms. Melanie. She's a friend of your daddy."

Removing his hood, an adorable boy emerged.

"Oh my, Suzanne! What handsome young man you have."

"This is Kyle, age five, my big afternoon kindergartner."

"It's a pleasure to meet you."

"Mommy, I'm starving!"

"Very well, you get rid of those wet things, and after you've changed into play clothes, I'll have a snack ready."

Kyle quickly disappeared down the hall.

"I suppose Ricky and JP were that way once."

"You knew both of the Sheridan boys?"

"Oh yes."

"I never knew Ricky. He'd died before John and I got engaged."

"I knew Ricky well. We both attended Farnsworth College. I really don't want to bore you now. Please pass me a cookie."

"Can you at least tell me why you want to see my husband today, and not some other time?"

Melanie's eyes began to tear. "It's our anniversary."

"Of what?"

"Ricky and I had gotten engaged on this date. We were to be wed shortly before his death. My infant daughter was only nine months old when he died, and she was given up for adoption two months later."

Just then, young Kyle returned and began munching away.

"Come, Melanie. Bring your tea, and we'll sit in the front parlor while my son feasts on his Twinkies and chips."

Suzanne suddenly felt closer to her new friend after she realized they could have been sisters-in-law if John's brother had lived. The two women sat across from each other in high wing-back chairs separated by a glass coffee table.

Melanie faced a beautifully painted portrait of Suzanne that hung over the fireplace. "Tell me about your painting."

"John did that of me shortly after he'd moved into my Watergate apartment.

We often comment about how well off I was from being a model and how poor he was from being an artist."

"I suppose things have improved for him from the looks of your lovely home."

"They have. John has just recently gotten a large commission to produce a series of presidential portraits for the Bicentennial Commission in Philadelphia.

He's there now finalizing the deal."

"Sounds wonderful, how about yourself, Suzanne?"

Laughing, she felt somewhat embarrassed by saying, "My hands earn more than my face."

"How so?"

"They've appeared in more television commercials than I can remember."

"I'm glad both of you are successful in your careers."

"Okay. Now tell me something wonderful that's happened in your world."

Lowering her eyes, she responded, "My treatment is finished, and I'm no longer on parole."

Suzanne's head spun as she wondered, "What kind of person did I just let into my house? Is she an ex-con? A drug offender, or what?" Trying to contain her emotions of fear, she calmly said, "I'm glad for you."

"Mommy!" came echoing from the kitchen.

"Melanie, please excuse me while I see what Kyle wants."

"Certainly," replied Melanie.

Suzanne got up and left the front room. She went into the kitchen and found another round of snacks for her vivacious son. She then directed him into the family room and turned on his favorite TV cartoons. When she got him settled, she returned to the parlor only to find Melanie and her multicolored umbrella gone.

She glanced over at the coffee table and saw what appeared to be a class ring placed in a center of the table. Picking it up, she saw the initials "R. E. S." on the class of '68 Sharpsburg High School ring. Just then, the doorbell chimed.

"Coming," she called. "Melanie, is that you?" she said as she opened the door.

"Not exactly, dear," said her husband. "I seemed to have misplaced my house key."

"Oh, John! Welcome home, honey." After they embraced in the doorway, she asked, "Did you see her?"

"Who, darling?"

"Melanie."

"Melanie who?

"Some young woman came by a little while ago asking to see you. She told me her name was Melanie Dulane. She said she knew both you and your brother from high school."

"Really! There was a girl named Melanie Dulane from Littlestown who used to run with Ricky."

"Well, she said she was finished with her treatment and off parole."

"Ah, now I remember, sweet Mel-an-ie. After I went off to Vietnam, my dear brother Ricky dated her and stole her heart. I was naturally curious. I never saw her again after Ricky's death. I wonder why she came by today."

"She told me it was her anniversary of being engaged to your brother."

"Man. Now that's a heavy trip."

"She reminded me a lot of a leftover Flower Child from the 1960s."

"Yeah. That's Melanie all right."

"Just a moment ago, Kyle called me back into the kitchen, and when I returned to the front room, she was gone."

"How strange."

"And John, she left this on our coffee table." She handed him the class ring.

"My brother's ring! I never knew what became of it. This is really a great gift to remember him by. Someday, I'll have to tell you the whole story . . . But now, I'm eager to see little Kyle."

Another quick kiss and after handing her his wet coat, he disappeared down the hall and into the family room. Suzanne sighed and glanced outside at the dripping raindrops off the trees and beyond to the deserted street. She did not see Melanie anywhere. "He sure didn't seem worried or anxious about her visit . . . and I'm wondering what her real story is. I guess he'll tell it to me sometime."

As the grandfather clock in the foyer struck four times, Melanie Dulane hailed the same taxi that brought John from the train station. Once inside, she told the driver to return to downtown Washington's Dupont Circle. Inside her sweater pocket was John's house key.

"Hold that picture out. Let me check these files if there's one on her."

"Bingo! Yes," he said while handing her the thinner file.

Jen's hand, for some unknown reason, began to tremble as she opened the file. "Look, here's a file on Melanie Dulane! Kyle, I don't know who this person is, but they sure are sending out strange vibes."

"Evidentially,"—he frowned—"that bitch still can to that from her grave."

File Eleven

Melanie Dulane ran and lived with a Kiki Flaund and some other girls named Moonbeam and Sunshine off campus in a commune two miles east of Farnsworth College.

Hippie Commune near Farnsworth College
September 1971

Farnsworth juniors, Ricky, Teddy, Joe, and Melanie's girlfriends Kiki, Sunshine, and Moonbeam were tripping out on LSD. Music by Iron Butterfly played loudly in the background while incense burned, giving off a pungent odor. A black light in one corner eerily illuminated several florescent-painted posters that were draped across the living room ceiling. A red lava lamp, sitting on an end table, slowly continued to bubble. The window shades were pulled down, completely blocking the midday sun, while all five of the acid eaters lay naked on old mattresses that were in the center of the room. They were entangled into a massive ball of purple glowing human flesh. Ricky had left and was collapsed on the living room sofa.

Melanie was upstairs rocking her five-month-old infant daughter to sleep who continued to cry. Loud music echoed through the entire old farmhouse.

The speaker's vibrations caused some of the old plaster to crack in places.

She put the baby on the bed and went downstairs. Empty beer cans were strewn everywhere in her path. Entering the living room, she became very agitated and called to her nude boyfriend, "Ricky! Please tell Joey or Kiki to turn that damn music off so I can get baby Jennifer to sleep."

Ricky stumbled to his feet and opened another door. He looked in on the nude bodies lying on a mattress. "Hey you, the whore upstairs is bitchin' about the music. She wants it turned off so she can trip out in peace."

Joey Henson, who appeared drunk and was about to snort some coke, said,

"Did you believe that shit from her?"

Kiki Flaund began laughing hysterically and said, "Tell her to check in to the fucking Travel Lodge over on Route 15 if she needs quiet."

Melanie remained alone in an upstairs bedroom watching out the window for any sign of pigs (police). Tears formed often as she continued to hear the commotion below. Tenderly, she rocked her now-sleeping infant daughter.

"Gee, I wonder if those were their codenames," Kyle asked while trying to get a mental image of the hippie commune community near the Farnsworth campus.

"I doubt it. It sounds pure drug-culture to me," Jen replied as she began walking around the bedroom examining this file.

"I know her! She's the one that was committed to the state hospital for being involved in my uncle Ricky's death."

"Really!"

"Jen, yeah. And look here. It's her girlfriend Kiki's file."

"How do you know that?"

"My mom—God rest her soul—knew these people and often wondered what ever happened to them."

"Jen, listen to me," Kyle said. "If she's the same Melanie that my parents knew, she was a real nutcase. After my daddy's death, she committed suicide."

"Well this file doesn't say all that," she replied, feeling that questions about her origins still remained unanswered.

"Let's see. Maybe something will turn up in this stack of files."

After a time, Kyle came running into the kitchen. "Jen! Get a load of this."

He presented her with two more folders that had different colored markings on the cover including a U.S. government authorization code that read "Property of U.S. Army—Top Secret Documents.

"Whose files are they?" she inquired.

With a look of disgust on his face, Kyle replied, "These both are on my daddy's old army buddy, Sergeant Peter Matavich."

"Oh Kyle! You've really found the can of worms now. It's against the law to be found with top secret military documents."

"I . . . know. But these hold the key to my daddy's past. I've never really knew the man except what my grandparents had told me. And I'm sure they never knew of his involvement in all of this."

"All right, I know that my daddy was a soldier in Vietnam. Let's see.

20

File Twelve

Peter Matavich had joined Lieutenant David Prestol's platoon about six months after JP Sheridan arrived. JP was assigned to introduce Peter and other new platoon members to the method of operations for a covert mission.

Each man in the platoon had been assigned certain responsibilities such as ammunition, weapons, provisions, transportation, heavy or light equipment, communications, scouting or mine/booby trap detection. JP was responsible for the safekeeping of recovered artifacts from enemy control and had been trained in communications.

Peter, on the other hand, was the mess cook. His training in the fast-food world was enough experience for Lieutenant Prestol to assign him that task.

Both JP and Peter were nearing their twentieth birthdays. The two men were assigned to the same unit and shared living quarters. That often meant a foxhole or tent. Peter was from the Midwest. He talked with a Ukrainian-Missouri accent.

Army rations were delivered by truck or flight-dropped. Peter maintained a tight control over the food provisions. It seemed like there was either a feast or a famine. The supply of food would last only about five days. Following that and prior to a replenishment, the platoon was reduced to eating their beloved C-rations or canned spam and beans at each meal.

Peter usually remained at the base camp with the provisions while the others were out jungle-hopping for VC targets. One day, the recon men returned at the base camp and could not locate Peter. Notice went out that he may have been taken captive by the VC. But just as a search-and-rescue party was being organized, Peter showed up at the camp with several apparently orphaned children and a cow on a leash.

The Red Cross quickly evacuated the children by chopper. The entire platoon was treated to a steak dinner that night that was reminiscent of days gone by.

Peter and JP remained good buddies throughout their war-time hitch.

After JP returned Stateside following the death of his older brother, Peter was transferred to Fort Douglas nearly a year later. There, he met and worked with the infamous doctor Colonel Travis Cummings, MD.

Dr. Cummings found Peter a receptive participant in his medical research project. Dr. Cummings often would talk to Peter in length about Lieutenant David Prestol's platoon and his working closely with Sergeant JP Sheridan.

Dr. Cummings then began to plot how he could use Peter to find JP Sheridan's location to arrest and interrogate him about the missing fortune.

What no one realized was JP had actually only handed all the money bags from Lieutenant David's Vietnam recovery operations, Colonel Cummings's research money, along with the drug sales from the six regional campuses to Professor Henry Prestol.

Henry laughed when one day JP found a stack of Mercantile deposit slips in the chemistry lab. Henry stated that he stashed the money somewhere and that these deposit slips were bogus. JP explained this fact once to Peter and that became an assumed lie according to the colonel.

Peter was mind-conditioned repeatedly during his time stationed at Fort Douglas. Dr. Cummings became more and more frustrated with Peter's inability and decided to double cross him.

Peter had met the folks over at Farnsworth College earlier on, shortly after he reported to Fort Douglas. Colonel Cummings informed the college that by February 1973, Peter Matavich was his choice to replace AWOL JP Sheridan.

Peter was conditioned to carry on JP's drug connections with the other six area campuses and gave all the collected money then to Colonel Cummings.

This was when, in a state of heightened anxiety and depression, Peter was able to secretly locate JP in Washington, D.C., and revealed Cummings's plot. Both JP and his fiancée, Suzanne, welcomed Peter and kept him hidden from the military at their Rose Hill home for about a week. During that time, a private wedding was held for JP and Suzanne. Peter was his best man and little Kyle celebrated his third birthday at that time.

Following the wedding, Peter informed the FBI and the U.S. Army about the colonel's covert operation using government money and drug sales for personal gain while serving in the military. An agent of the colonel secretly had wiretapped the conversation and notified the colonel about his trader.

The doctor then contacted the AWOL research soldier, Peter, and offered him clemency if he would return back to Fort Douglas. Peter, having left JP's home, met the doctor's agent on his own at the designated location in D.C. Once inside the military vehicle, Peter was restrained and injected. Peter was never to be seen nor heard from again. Dr. Cummings quickly programmed each of his guards to overdose. This action assured that his assets would be preserved before being taken prisoner by the military.

"That's an odd name, Kyle. Who's he?" called Jen from the kitchen. "Was he some sort of foreign agent?"

"Not quite. He's someone my daddy knew from Vietnam."

"Did he ever attend Farnsworth?"

"I believe so, for a short while, after he returned from Vietnam and must have been stationed at Fort Douglas."

Jen asked Kyle to try and locate Peter Matavich. Once the information operator located the number, he called and introduced himself. His wife was curious about the call.

"I am the son of your husband's best friend from Vietnam," Kyle said, feeling proud.

After remembering about her late husband mentioning that he was the best man at JP and Suzanne Sheridan's wedding, she then recalled hearing about JP's three-year-old son named Kyle.

Kyle began politely asking her when her late husband had met his daddy.

"From what I remember, they were assigned the same platoon under Captain David Prestol. Now there was quiet a character, I'd say."

"How so?" asked Kyle with determined interest.

"He had the young men under his command constantly going on dangerous nighttime raids, looking for and recovering those so-called lost artifacts."

"What were they?" asked Kyle.

"Your daddy and Peter must have recovered over a million dollars' worth of gold statues and jewelry that had been stolen by the Khmer Rouge from the state museum in Saigon in a robbery back in the late 1960s. The government of South Vietnam had offered handsome rewards for the recovery of those stolen items. It appeared that Captain Prestol cut a deal with the Saigon government to use his men and equipment to do the job."

"Were they successful?" asked Kyle.

"I believe so."

"Did they become rich?

"I don't know. That money was sent home to his brother who had it deposited into some mysterious Mercantile Bank account. It seems that later, the men who contributed to that account were going to set up some sort of new chemical company."

"Did your husband or my daddy ever get stocks or benefits from this company?"

"No! Because after the captain died in Vietnam, your dad and Peter returned home to work and attend Farnsworth College. My husband once told me that your dad had the account number, but it turned out to be bogus. That money remains hidden somewhere, and since all the men who contributed to the account are gone, no one else has been able to find it for over twenty years now."

She continued, "After your dad left Farnsworth Campus in early 1973, Peter continued his operations with an army colonel Cummings. The colonel began to harass my husband, figuring your dad had told him everything about the missing money. My Peter notified the army after becoming terminally ill, and that evil colonel was arrested and sent to prison. No one ever mentioned anything more about it. And now it seems like only God knows where all that money is."

"My fiancée and I are trying to solve another mystery from that time period. We're both attending Farnsworth College as graduate students. Lately, we seem to have made several individuals here very nervous. And I really don't know why."

"Kyle, be very careful and watch your step. Strange things happened on that campus twenty some years ago. Peter told me about your dad and his brother's extensive drug dealing."

"What!" cried Kyle.

"Your dad and uncle were really involved with the distribution of a hallucinogenic called Sernyl. It was really a powerful mind-altering drug. It was the cause of all those poor student's suicides."

"Excuse me. Are we talking about the same JP Sheridan?"

"Yes, young man, we are."

Feeling almost betrayed by her comments, Kyle asked, "Is there anything else I should know about my notorious daddy?"

"Only that Peter often questioned your dad about where he spent all his money. It seemed like he was always broke. In fact, my Peter lent him some money several times when your dad seemed to be down on his luck."

"Well, Mrs. Matavich. I'm sorry that I never met your husband as an adult."

"Oh, you couldn't have. He spent the last ten years in a comatose state at Lebanon State Hospital. He passed in 1984."

"I'm so sorry, Mrs. Matavich. I didn't know. Goodbye."

Kyle hung up the phone and remained seated as Jen walked into the room. "Kyle, what's wrong? Wasn't she helpful?"

He began to cry saying, "My daddy, Uncle Ricky, and Peter Matavich were all drug dealers!"

"What the hell?" cried a shocked Jen.

"That's what her late husband had said to her before he became ill and had to be committed to the state mental hospital."

"Oh my god! Darling, that may be why people are so suddenly different toward us when you introduce yourself as the son of JP Sheridan."

Jen got up and said, "Kyle, I'm going to fix us some coffee. Please pick up this mess when you're finished."

"Sure. No problem. How about after that we shower together and have a relaxing Monday evening?"

Smiling, she told him, "Sounds inviting." Then continuing, she told her lover, "Kyle, I love you, and I don't want anything ever happen to you. Please don't keep digging up the past. Remember you've already had two warnings, and I'm giving you another."

"But how will I ever know?"

"Listen to me, darling," she said while taking hold of his hand.

"Know that your daddy became a great artist during his lifetime, and his work will always be remembered from the bicentennial celebration. That was his crowning project. He served his country in that way, not as some drugged-up, robot-style security guard in some damn perverted army medical research experiment."

"Yeah, you're right. I have good memories of my daddy."

"That's right. Now here's your coffee, and let's spend time after this making some serious love."

21

Day Eight
Wednesday
September 21, 1994

Shortly after 9:00 a.m., Kyle called the Mercantile Bank in Harrisburg with what he believed was a lost account number. The friendly bank manager searched their file records and found no such account or lockbox that matched. Looking under the various names of Alexander, Cummings, Prestol, and even Sheridan, there was no evidence of any former account. Kyle appreciated the information and hung up the phone. Tearfully, he became more frustrated and said, "I believe it's time, Jen, that we paid my dear grandparents a visit. They never seemed to talk much about the past."

"It's Tuesday. Why do you think they'll tell us something today about twenty-some years ago?" she asked with a pleading and anxious look.

"These files tell only part of their stories. They lived through each day and must have kept up with their son's activities."

"You're a dreamer. My adoptive parents never knew where I was or who I was running with, only when I told them."

"I don't know. Maybe we can sit down with them this afternoon and actually get to the truth regarding my daddy, JP Sheridan, and my uncle, Ricky Sheridan, Jr.'s involvement here at Farnsworth College."

"Their answers could really help us at this point."

"I'll call and see if we could drop by later."

The historic town of Gettysburg was about a half hour drive from the campus. Kyle's grandparents lived in a Civil-War-era two-story brick house on Baltimore Street. The Sheridan family had made Gettysburg their home since before World War II.

"Well, here we are."

"Kyle, the house is lovely. And the neighborhood probably resembled the way it looked during the Civil War, very quaint."

Kyle's grandmother, Mary, answered the doorbell. "Welcome, home, Kyle. And this must be your friend, Jennifer. It's so nice to finally meet you. Kyle's already told me all about you."

Looking at him with a frown, Jen said, "I hope he said nice things?"

"Why of course, Jen. Only nice things."

"Is the old bastard, uh, I mean, Grandpa around?" asked Kyle.

"He'll be home soon enough. I paged him on the job site that you all were coming by this afternoon."

"Grandma, Jen and I have just found some old files on different people who attended Farnsworth College in the late 1960s and early 1970s. Daddy and Uncle Ricky were mentioned in those files along with classmates and faculty members."

"These files appear to be very secretive. No one on campus will talk to us about them," replied Jen.

"I see. So you kids drove all the way here to ask your grandpa and me questions about our, God rest their souls, sons." She began to weep.

"Please, Grandma. Don't let this upset you. We're just trying to find the truth."

Wiping her tears away, she said, "The truth is what has caused such pain. The stories told us painted only what we wanted to believe. There's plenty that the army won't tell us because both Ricky and JP and their friends somehow became involved in a secret army research project."

"All right, forget that part of the story," Kyle told his grandma with a look of disappointment.

"Would you like me to tell you some stories about when your father and his brother were younger and we were all a happy family growing up in the 1960s?"

"That would be nice, Mrs. Sheridan. Everything we've read so far had been so disturbing and depressing," replied Jennifer.

"Come, both of you. Lunch is ready and your grandpa won't be along for a while."

"Thanks, Grandma. I love you and Grandpa," said Kyle as he gave her a kiss on her cheek.

During lunch, Mary relayed background information to Jennifer about their decision to raise Kyle following the loss of his parents.

"With our two sons, Ricky and JP gone, little Kyle, at age five, was a new source of life for his grandpa and me. We all lived in this house and have always been a Christian family and had attended church regularly. Richard, Sr., still owns a successful construction business while I'm a retired English high school teacher. This family grew together then was pulled in different directions during the turbulent late 1960s."

"That's terrible," Jen said.

Mary continued, "I experienced difficulty teaching my own sons in English classes. Both brothers seemed to be preoccupied with girls, sex, and social activities. This bothered me and my husband. That made the brothers frustrated. Kyle, from high school on, your daddy's nickname was JP. He became used to being called that way. He seemingly admired his older brother Ricky since they were children."

Turning to Jennifer, she said, "JP was a year younger than Ricky and appeared to demonstrate artistic abilities early on. Ricky was labeled a gifted student and became a high school jock. A strapping six-footer, his favorite sport was basketball."

"I didn't know that," said Kyle as he continued to eat his tuna fish sandwich.

"JP, although feeling he would remain shorter in height, never publicly displayed his dislike or jealously for Ricky's achievements, but I knew he resented Ricky. Both young men were successful in attracting girls. One particular girl whom Ricky really enjoyed her companionship was this certain tiny bopper named Melanie Dulane from Littlestown."

"Yeah, I do recall her," Kyle said with distain.

"JP also liked Melanie but kept his distance while she ran with Ricky. Kyle, your father's school grades were average or slightly below.

Whenever there was a big test coming up, he would employ Ricky as his tutor. While in high school, JP followed closely his brother's process of getting a student deferment and finally his acceptance into Farnsworth College."

"That's very interesting, Mrs. Sheridan," commented Jen.

"With a fair scholastic record and a very impressive sports background, Ricky was welcomed with open arms in Farnsworth in September 1968 as a member of the college's class of '72. In the late spring of 1968, JP considered dropping out of high school because of the lure of overseas travel and adventure. He actually had an interest in joining the merchant marines. He still needed convincing and Ricky didn't seem very interested in JP's personal dreams. He was a very good artist who liked to draw and paint. Often he would go on field trips alone to find a quiet place to be one with nature."

Kyle's Grandma continued, "He loved to travel on foot throughout the historic battlefield. Blossoming dogwoods made this teenage artist admire the beauty of nature's springtime show. JP had a favorite spot from which he did many drawings and watercolors. His place must have been quiet and peaceful. Before him loomed the massive rock formation that had been named Devil's Den. Immediately to his left was an area referred to as the Valley of Death, with its meandering stream below Little Round Top. That area was the scene of fierce fighting on the second day of the battle."

She paused and lamented, "JP seemed to be drawn often to this corner of the historic Civil War Gettysburg battlefield. Nothing there had changed for over 109 summers since those brave men in Union blue and Confederate gray clashed in that terrible battle that began on July 1, 1863."

"There's a ton of history in these parts," added Kyle.

"JP felt anxious when his brother Ricky was graduating from high school and heading off to college by summer's end, and he decided, against our wishes, to drop out of high school."

Kyle and Jen continued to listen to Mary's recollections with intense fascination.

22

Farnsworth College Campus
June 1969

Richard Sheridan, Sr., his wife, Mary, and long-haired hippie-looking son, Ricky, walked past a sign that said, "Freshmen Orientation Today."

"Well, Ricky," said his pop. "Your mother and I are very proud that you are able to attend this beautiful campus to get your education. With your ten-thousand-dollar scholarship, you are completely paid up through your bachelor's degree. This college, with its high standards and excellent facility, will be something to carry with you the rest of your life."

Ricky looked at his father strangely and mumbled, "Right on, Pop."

Mary told Kyle and Jen, "JP tagged along with my husband and me to tour the campus prior to the start of Ricky's freshman semester. While there, during the last weekend of July 1968, he and Ricky met many of Farnsworth's faculty members." Continuing, she said,

"My long-haired Ricky had planned to become chemistry major. I remember JP watched, for the first time, how Ricky and a certain chemistry professor named Henry Prestol talked in length about the ideologies on our involvement in Vietnam. That professor was really hell-bent against our government sending all those thousands of young Americans over there," his grandma proclaimed. "Kyle, your daddy probably felt very uncomfortable and definitely out of place since he had dropped out of high school and already had been drafted for a tour of duty in the army. After mentioning that fact, Professor Prestol commented that his brother David was a gung-ho Officer in the army and was a platoon commander in Vietnam. JP told us later how he was struck odd that this man who was totally against the police action that even his own brother supported."

"Now I see where you inherited you're study habits," laughed Jen.

"Let me back up a moment," Mary told them. "Kyle, In June 1969, your uncle Ricky graduated from Gettysburg High School while his sweetheart Melanie Dulane graduated from Littlestown High. Your daddy, as I said earlier, was a year younger and decided to take a break from school. That's when he shortly had gotten his draft notice. There's something I just remembered from his youth."

"What would that be, Grandma?" asked Kyle.

"I remember him telling me that one day before Ricky's graduation, he was out on the Gettysburg battlefield doing some sketching and had discovered an area where some hippie young people had been using drugs. He also discovered his brother's class ring lying in the dirt and connected his brother Ricky to the drug scene. JP didn't tell us just then and returned the ring to his grateful brother."

She then recalled, "At the beginning of August 1969, Ricky and Melanie were accepted at Farnsworth College. Afterwards, Ricky met his roommate, Teddy Lancer, and they became good friends."

"Oh my! That's a familiar name lately," commented Jennifer.

"Ms. Melanie's dorm mate was a hippie named Kiki something."

"Yes," Jen said. "She's now the widow of Dean Joseph Henson."

"Kiki must have been the one of those students to introduce Melanie and Ricky to some campus hippies and drug users," Kyle theorized.

"When your daddy dropped out of high school before graduation, both my husband and I were furious. We both knew he had really developed as a young artist and even had his eyes on the Maryland Institute of Art. However, his father thought that was a bad choice. JP struggled to please his pop knowing that Ricky could never do wrong and he seemingly could never do what was right."

Jen sighed, "I've heard of families like that."

Mary continued, "By the end of June '69, JP and his pop were not speaking. Ricky returned home for the weekend from college and got into it over JP's not obeying his pop's wishes. Kyle, your uncle Ricky believed that your daddy should have worked construction after he'd dropped out and earned college money that way. JP told everyone that he'd been drafted in the army and left in a huff."

Fort Bragg, North Carolina
July 1969

John Paul Sheridan and other eighteen-year-olds got off a bus with a nearby sign pointing "Recruit Receiving Entrance." The group was met by a master sergeant wearing fatigues and carrying a roster list.

"Sheridan, John Paul from Gettysburg."

"Here, sir," replied JP quietly.

The sergeant smiled and said, "Son, I didn't hear you."

"Here, sir."

"I still didn't hear you, little punk!"

He then yelled back, "Present, sir!"

In a louder voice, the sergeant replied, "Get your dumb ass over here with the rest of those worthless scumbags!"

JP scrambled to join the line of raw recruits. The sergeant then yelled out again, "For the next ten weeks, I'm your mommy, daddy, your old grandpappy, your high school principal, and anyone else who corrupted your little fucking heads. You're mine, babies! Me, and your Uncle Sam, will change your shit-brain civilian attitudes to a more focused, positive U.S. Army attitude! Is that understood, ass wipes?"

Each of the recruit yelled nervously, "Yes, sir!"

"Now, girlies, everyone turn to your left and follow your lovable sergeant into that fucking building. You bunch of lowlives. Move it! That's an order!"

"Kyle, I feel really sorry for your daddy. It must have been a difficult time for him," replied Jen.

Mary then said, "Ricky returned to Farnsworth, and by the spring of 1970, he had befriended Professor Prestol in the chemistry department. Ricky, we believe, was forced to do the professor's dirty work. That man was the principal organizer of all the campus antiwar protests and personally attended marches and demonstrations against our involvement in Vietnam. He was a radical and totally un-American."

"Maybe he was a communist," commented Kyle.

"By this time, the draft was reinstated and the protests became more aggressive and ugly," said the grandmother. "Your late uncle Ricky told us about one account I can remember."

Farnsworth College Quad
May 1970

Once the announcement of the shootings of several demonstrating students at Kent State University in Ohio was on the news, the bells tolled from the college chapel bell tower. Angry Farnsworth students quickly assembled in the quad area from all parts of the campus.

Students glanced toward the administration building and saw Dean Tricia Alexander returning their gaze from the third-floor corner window.

They saw clearly she was holding a telephone.

"Yes, Colonel Cummings. Our three juniors Teddy Lancer, Joey Henson, and Ricky Sheridan, Jr., are doing a superb job. They're inciting the crowd this very moment with their loudspeakers. When they turn this peaceful antiwar protest violent, your newly trained security forces will have plenty of new talent for your research program. Your Operation CAVE is the best thing that ever to hit our little quiet campus. I can't thank you enough."

"Why thank you, Dean Alexander. I'll move my people into position as soon as possible. They already have their orders. I'll have my driver bring me over within fifteen minutes to supervise."

"That'll be fine, Colonel. Just make sure our student leaders are identified for the press before they're brought to Fort Douglas."

"Of course, we want this confrontation totally covered by our local press. All of the arresting officers are graduates of my CAVE program. Their conditioning is complete."

After calling security to break up the scene with tear gas, Dean Alexander smiled peering out the window. Everyone ran in panic. Military troops, combined with campus police, began arresting targeted student demonstrators.

They yelled and cursed her generation for bringing them to this confrontation.

The crowd then quickly dispersed from the campus quad area.

The dean, feeling again relaxed, opened her desk drawer and took out a ledger. Upon opening the book, she reviewed the sources and several millions of dollars that had been deposited into her Mercantile trust account.

"I can't imagine," Jen lamented, shaking her head in disbelief.

"Kyle, your daddy graduated from basic training in the late summer of ' 69. He came home for a week before shipping out for Vietnam but stayed at his friend's house."

Jen then mentioned, "You and your husband must have been confronted with the situation that each son was off defending different principles. Ricky defended his right to the First Amendment's tolerance of free speech and the right to demonstrate while his brother, JP, was actually defending his country's honor in an undeclared war to preserve a small democracy in Southeast Asia."

"That must have been a tough call for you and Grandpa because you loved both of your sons," said Kyle. "Jen read that the college provided both student and professor volunteers for the army's secret medical research project.

"Yes, and I've always suspected a lot of drugs and money changed hands in process. You all had better wait until your grandpa arrives. Then let him answer those types of questions."

"Sure, Grandma, whatever you say. Oh, do you mind if I show Jen around the house?"

"Not at all, if you would be interested in showing your lady any old photos, the album is up in the attic on top of some boxes."

"Sure, we love attics." Jen winked at a blushing Kyle. "Thanks so much for the lunch. It really was delicious."

"Thanks for sharing the stories, Grandma," said Kyle.

After walking through the dimly lighted house and seeing several pieces of wonderfully hand-carved antique furniture, Kyle opened the door to the attic. "Watch your step. These stairs are narrow."

Once Kyle and Jen were able to stand upright in the jam-packed, junk-filled attic, she immediately walked over to the rounded turret and looked out the curved glass window at Baltimore Street below.

"This place is so cool! And that's simply the best view of this town."

"I used to play up here a lot as a young boy. I pretended to be a knight in that neat castle turret. Ah, over there's the photo album."

"God! What an exciting time it must have been to live through. Kyle, don't you agree?"

"Yeah, sort of. You know, the part about the hippie's communal living made me feel all horny, you know, lots of naked girls lying around in your pad doing nothing but drugs and having sex with multiple partners."

"No. It doesn't appeal to me at all. I like our privacy and just you in my bed."

"All right, my Ms. Traditionalist! You're on as soon as we're through here."

Jen began to flip through the pages as Kyle's attention was drawn toward a large black steamer trunk in the corner. Reading the tag attached near the padlock, it read "Master Sergeant John P. Sheridan, U.S. Army 3-13-761-023."

"Jen! Over here! It's my daddy's footlocker."

"It looks like the trunk has never been opened by the looks of that old rusted padlock."

"No one evidently has the key. Hmmm."

23

Supply Depot, Fort Bragg
1986

After spending most of the day supervising a work party of young recruit privates, the quartermaster tired. The assigned task was to empty out a large storage room nearly filled to capacity with steamer trunks and footlockers.

Many had seemingly been here for years. For some reason or another, the army considered them "lost in transit" and never claimed.

Each trunk was heavy. The young handlers suffered greatly in the unairconditioned building in July. Each trunk's owner information was recorded by the quartermaster and handed to a sergeant. He, in turn, took the names and entered them into a main computer in the supply office. Many of the names on the printout showed the owners were killed in action in Vietnam.

When this occurred, the personal possessions were usually sent directly home. However, with so many soldiers reported missing in action or the remains unidentified, their trunks remained stored here.

As two privates lifted down another trunk, the quartermaster read the name "Master Sergeant John P. Sheridan, U.S. Army 3-13-761-023."

"Sergeant, I've heard of this man. He was one of Captain David Prestol's boys in Special Forces!"

"Yes, sir. My printout indicates he was not killed in Vietnam but died in 1976 in Washington, D.C."

"Who's his next of kin, Sergeant?"

"This shows his parents are the survivors and live in Gettysburg, Pennsylvania."

"Fine, Corporal, over here."

"Sir, what is it?"

"Have these two privates escort you to shipping and personally see that this trunk is properly delivered to the Sheridan family."

"Certainly, sir, it'll be an honor."

All the men saluted each other, and the corporal saw that JP's trunk was sent within four hours.

Several days later, the doorbell rang on Baltimore Street in Gettysburg.

Two army officers stood at the door.

"Mrs. Richard Sheridan, Sr.?"

"Yes. What is it?" replied Kyle's grandmother, Mary.

"Pardon us, ma'am. We've come to deliver your son's, Master Sergeant John Sheridan, footlocker."

"Well, I'll be! The army had told us that it was lost, and that caused my son—God rest his soul—great anguish."

"This trunk was located recently in Fort Bragg by the quartermaster and his work party."

"I see. There's no one here but me today. My husband and grandson are out of town. Would you men mind putting this trunk up in my attic?"

"No, ma'am. It's an honor to carry Sergeant Sheridan's possessions. We understand he was highly decorated from Vietnam."

"Yes, he was. He had the Silver and Bronze Star medals along with a Purple Heart and the Army Commendation medal."

"You must have been extremely proud of those accomplishments."

"I suppose we were at the time, but now they don't mean much without him around."

"Understand, ma'am. Please lead the way to your attic."

The two young officers struggled somewhat with the awkward trunk. Mary directed where to place it and then closed the door behind them. No one had the key, so the trunk remained unopened in the attic for the past eight years.

"Oh, Kyle, you grandpa's here. You kids come on down."

"Be right there, Grandma."

Kyle entered the kitchen followed closely by Jennifer.

"Well, about time you came to visit us, boy!"

"It's been a while, Grandpa. I'm sorry."

"It's been a long damn while, boy!" Then turning toward Jen, he asked, "Who's this? Is she a new love interest?"

"No, sir. She's my fiancée, Jen."

"I'm Jennifer Howser, Mr. Sheridan. How do you do?"

"Hmmmm. Kyle, your grandma tells me you're asking some more goddamn questions about your late daddy."

"Yes, sir, I recently found some old files on campus and wondered if you could tell us any more facts."

"That fact is the goddamn army has all your answers. Not me or your grandma. Is that understood?"

"But, Grandpa, there may be a cover-up or a conspiracy or something. Dean Henson was murdered in his office the other day by a fellow who was just was released from prison."

Jumping from his chair, the old man pinned Kyle's head against the kitchen cabinets and yelled, "Listen up! You smart-aleck college punk! For the last time, there's nothing to talk about! Understand, boy?"

"Yes . . . yes, Grandfather."

"Let him go!" screamed Jennifer. "You're hurting him!"

"Come on, Pa. They've gotten your message," replied Mary.

Loosening his grip on Kyle, Richard broke down and began to shout through his tears. Displaying years of frustration in his voice, he said, "Ricky and JP are dead! Do you understand that! You little bastard! Nothing you two can do or find will ever change that! Go away! Leave your grandma and me to ourselves. At least, we can live our lives without being harassed as we were before."

Mary held her sobbing husband in her arms. "See what you started? Just go away as he said."

"Sorry. Come on, Jen. We'll leave."

Kyle and Jen held hands tightly as they reentered the sun-drenched sidewalk in front of the old brick house.

"They do know the truth . . . but for some damn reason, they seemed almost scared to talk."

"Kyle, do you think the army's still involved with Farnsworth College?"

"It's difficult to say at this point because the only person from that period we've met has been Dr. Cummings. Professors Hill and Moore are much younger and haven't been there that long."

"But, darling, a former medical doctor is not usually in charge of current military operations since he appears to no longer be connected with them."

"Well, he certainly was twenty-two years ago, and I would wager money he's somehow involved even in today's time.

District Courtroom
Frederick, Maryland
January 1972

Richard Sheridan, Sr., his wife, Mary, and their youngest son, Master Sergeant John P. Sheridan, USA, remained seated and silent during the trial of Melanie Dulane.

Richard hugged his crying wife while JP intently stared at Melanie. The courtroom was quiet as His Honor began to speak, "Let me remind the court that Ms. Dulane is accused of causing the death of Ricky Sheridan, Jr., with a lethal dose of tainted LSD. The court will now hear from the noted psychologist and Farnsworth professor Dr. William Gray."

The crowded courtroom turned its silent attention to him.

"Your Honor, speaking on behalf of Ms. Dulane, I must also tell you that since she has been under my care for the past month, it is my recommendation that she remain confined for further psychological evaluations because of her past drug addiction history."

The judge then ordered, "Bailiff, bring the defendant before the bench."

Melanie was escorted before the judge.

"Ms. Dulane, you have been found guilty of the premeditated death by drug overdose of Ricky Sheridan, Jr., who resided with you in your commune near Farnsworth College. This court accepts Dr. Gray's evaluation and has determined that you were indeed insane from drug use at the time of the occurrence. The taking of hallucinogenic substances was a reckless act. You are hereby ordered to be further confined to the state mental facility at Lebanon for an undisclosed period of time for psychological evaluation. It is furthermore ordered that your infant daughter, Jennifer, currently in foster care, be given up for immediate adoption."

"Thank you, Your Honor," replied Dr. Gray.

Melanie broke down and shouted, "It's not fair! I'm not responsible for Ricky's death. Ask his brother, soldier boy, JP Sheridan. Let him tell you how his tainted drugs killed my Ricky!"

With that statement, JP jumped to his feet and exclaimed, "It's a lie, Your Honor! This woman is burned- out on drugs herself. I was in Vietnam, serving my country, at the time of my older brother's death."

The judge hit his gavel and sternly said, "Enough! Quiet! Order in this court!"

Melanie was led away, struggling in handcuffs as the courtroom emptied.

A short time later, outside the courthouse, Colonel Travis Cummings, MD, and Master Sergeant Sheridan entered a military car and drove away.

JP's parents commented to each other about how distant he seemed during the trial. "It was as if he was in another world," Mary said to her husband.

"I just wish we could spend some time with him again and really find out what happened to our Ricky."

"The army knows what happened to poor Ricky," sobbed Mary.

"Come on, there's nobody left to answer our questions," Richard commented to his wife as he closed the car door and drove off.

"Excuse me, Colonel Cummings," JP inquired. "Sir, I understand that I am report to the state college in the morning for a meeting with their dean."

"Correct, mister," said the colonel in a firm tone. "Is there a problem?"

"Sir, their dean recently was implicated in a money-laundering operation, and I do not have the Intelligence Background Report on his successor."

"You'll have it before you leave. Anything else?" asked the colonel, eyeing him with suspicion.

"No, sir. Everything's under control."

"How much have you collected so far this week?"

"I've gotten one hundred and seventy-five thousand dollars, sir, from the nearby six colleges."

"Nice," smiled the colonel.

24

Day Nine
Thursday
September 22, 1994

This morning, neither Kyle nor Jen had class scheduled at the campus. They returned to the remaining files on their kitchen table. The first file mentioned Kyle's daddy.

Fort Douglas
January 1972

Sergeant John Sheridan hung up the phone and sat alone in his barracks' office. He felt very tired as he continued to unsuccessfully track the location of his missing steamer trunk.

"That damn trunk has everything I own in it, including the fucking bank account number," he thought to himself.

The pencil he held had just drawn another line through the last name on the list of army facilities that received overseas deliveries. He felt utter despair and helplessness about not being able to access the account. He was the sole survivor. His older brother, Ricky, had just overdosed in November, Professor Henry Prestol disappeared last June, and a Saigon prostitute had murdered Captain David Prestol before JP came home. He firmly believed that Colonel 125 Cummings, Dr.

William Gray, and a new individual named Joey Henson all want access to Henry and his Mercantile Bank account money.

Within a short time, the phone rang, and the caller requested his presence at once. He left the barracks and walked across the snow-covered base until he reached the medical lab building.

Entering the facility, he immediately noticed another group of hippie Farnsworth College students sitting on a bench in the lobby. Dr. William Gray cordially greeted him, and then they entered a side office and closed the door.

"What's up, Dr. Gray?" asked JP.

"Sergeant, there's been a change in our plans. The college reported that two more of our programmed students committed suicide yesterday in their dorm rooms."

"Good God! How terrible is that!"

"And that's not all."

"What do you mean?"

"One of those students managed to smuggle a letter off campus, and it turned up in his congressman's mailbox in Washington, D.C."

"That's some serious shit!"

"The Congressman called me this morning. He said that this note mentioned that Farnsworth College was investigating an internal problem of serious drug use. I explained to him that these radical students would write or say anything to undermine our expanded, all-voluntary medical research.

"Was the congressman satisfied?"

"He seemed to be . . . Except now, he wants to meet and talk with that student, and he's one that just overdosed."

"What do you suggest, Dr. Gray?"

"The colonel, our associate Joey Henson, and I think you should go to Washington and pretend to be that student."

"Why the fuck does it have to be me?"

"You are the same age as the student who just died. And you know enough about this damn operation to save all our asses from a full-blown congressional or FBI investigation."

"Would that put a stop to all this madness?"

"Sergeant Sheridan, I'm begging you. If you do us this favor, all of your late brother's work will not be lost, and that fortune will remain intact."

"Huh. And what about those damn kids in the hallway?"

"I just finished profiling and screening them to enter our latest research project. They seem excited at the prospect."

"Yeah." He laughed. "It's an easy course and always gives them a passing grade. Go ahead and burn their brains too. You'll only have a lot more suicides to explain, Dr. Gray."

"Sergeant, you're right. But for now, we must continue. Follow me to the lab, and I'll get your injection ready.

Jen picked up another file and said, "Kyle, there's a file here on Dr. William Gray, PhD. Remember, he's the one that Dean Alexander had fired."

"Hold on! I've heard that name before," replied Kyle with concern.

"I believe he is the same guy my mom used to see in D.C. for her depression before my parents' death. I must have just turned five when things got pretty weird around my house. Mom suspected my daddy was cheating or something like that."

File Thirteen
Union Train Station
Washington, D.C.
May 1976

Dr. William Gray again agreed to meet Suzanne Sheridan in the train station cafe located on the lower level. Dr. Gray was only there a few minutes when she arrived.

"Suzanne, over there looks like a quiet spot."

"That'll do fine. Please tell the waiter that I'd like a glass of white wine."

Dr. Gray motioned to the waiter and said, "White wine and a scotch on the rocks."

"Oh, Dr. Gray, I'm really beginning to feel the pressure of knowing that something serious is going on behind my back."

"Are you absolutely certain that your husband is involved, or is it just a hunch?"

"I . . . don't know. He's been acting so secretive lately that I know he's up to something. You see, Dr. Gray, we always talk about everything. We really do have good communication in our marriage. But now, it's like he's become a completely different person."

"Ah. Here we are," he told her while accepting the drinks from the waiter.

"Here, maybe this will make you feel better."

"What I need is solid proof."

"No, what you need is to confront him and find out exactly what's going on."

"I suppose you're right. I could waste a lot of precious time trying to chase him all over town. After all, he does still come home every night and plays with young Kyle."

"It sounds to me like young Kyle is pretty important in his life."

"His son is everything." She began to sob. "And if he were to leave, Kyle's little heart would be broken forever."

"Sounds like yours would be too."

"Yes . . . but there's got to be a good explanation for his recent behavior."

"When did you first suspect something was wrong?" he asked Suzanne.

"After his return from Philadelphia last week, he tells me he had gone there to meet members of the Bicentennial Committee for a review of his preliminary sketches. This commission was very important to him. His presidential portraits will be used in a lot of the celebration promotions."

"That's some honor. But tell me what exactly did he do to raise your suspicions?"

"He came home with a thick envelope. When I asked him what was in it, he laughed and said it contained his winnings from Atlantic City."

"Did it?"

"No. The envelope contained his high school yearbook. But it was not his graduation year. It was from the year earlier. The year his older brother, Ricky, had graduated."

"I . . . don't follow exactly. Your husband goes on a business trip and returned home with his brother's high school yearbook."

"Don't you see? John must have met someone at the meeting who knew his late brother."

"All right, so he meets someone who knew his brother."

"No John's brother died under mysterious circumstances during his senior year at Farnsworth College. My husband, at the time was in the army, stationed in Vietnam, when that occurred. He's been trying to find out the real truth ever since he returned home in November 1971 to attend his brother's funeral and attend the trial of his accused killer."

"Perhaps a new lead appeared in Philadelphia, and he's trying to follow up on it. That could explain his behavior this week."

"But, Dr. Gray, John must still learn to accept the courtroom verdict and leave his brother's insane killer to the caretakers at the Lebanon State Hospital."

"My god! Suzanne, I worked at that very institution as a clinical psychologist for the past four years?"

With a look of horror on her face, she said, "I had no idea. Perhaps you may have even come to know this terrible person who destroyed my husband's family."

"Do you recall the patient's name?" he asked with concern.

"My husband called her Melanie something, and that she had dated his late brother, Ricky Sheridan, Jr."

"Could it possibly be a former patient of mine named Melanie Dulane?"

"Why yes! That was her name!"

"Melanie Dulane was a woman who was consumed with a hatred of someone she often called JP."

"Oh, my dear Jesus! Dr. Gray! That's my husband's nickname from high school!"

Dr. Gray took hold of her trembling hands and looked with compassion into her eyes and said, "What I'm about to tell you may upset you even more.

I'm so sorry to say that I recently got a message that Ms. Melanie Dulane had overpowered her nurse and escaped from that mental hospital. To my knowledge, she's still at large."

"She's what? Oh god! No! No! No!" shouted a disbelieving Suzanne as the Union Station visitors and boarding train passengers looked at her hysterical outbursts with compassion.

Kyle and Jen then decided to drive back over to his grandparents' home. They had both agreed it was time to open his late daddy's footlocker. During the drive back to Gettysburg, Kyle began telling Jen, "According to my grandma, my uncle Ricky became reclusive and despondent for several months. His family was concerned about his health during his senior fall semester of 1971.

25

The decision was jointly made to return to Kyle's grandparents' home and finally open his daddy's steamer trunk. With the historic town of Gettysburg in sight, Kyle continued telling Jen what he could remember, "The following year, Ricky even got kicked off the varsity football squad in October '72. By Thanksgiving, he had returned home complaining of sight problems. My grandparents admitted him to the Gettysburg Memorial Hospital. Ricky apparently died of kidney failure three days later. His girlfriend was the arrested and accused of giving him the tainted drugs."

"That's some sad story. Your uncle Ricky seemed to have a lot going for him, and he threw it all away on drugs," lamented Jen.

Parking the '69 Mustang in front of his grandparents' house, Kyle commented, "No one seems to be home. I do have a door key. Come on."

"The house looks deserted."

"Jen, check over there!" he said, pointing to the garage. "Funny. Their car's still here."

Kyle opened the front door, and together they entered the foyer.

"Hello. Anyone home?" called Jen.

"Guess not. Jen, answers we seek have got to be inside daddy's steamer trunk."

Kyle and Jen climb the wide stairs to the second floor then proceed up the narrow steps into the attic. The antique grandfather clock began to gently chime.

U.S. Army Headquarters, Tokyo, Japan
November 30, 1971

Sergeant JP Sheridan, now aged twenty-two, entered the chaplain's office and saluted. The Protestant chaplain returned his salute.

"At ease, son."

"What is it, sir?"

"I've just received notice from your parents that your older brother, Ricky, has just died from a drug overdose."

"Oh god, no! How can it be?" JP cried out in anguish.

"His girlfriend is in custody and will likely be charged."

With nearly four years of Vietnam service behind him and a promising army career being obtainable, Sergeant Sheridan's life in an instant was changed forever. He began to cry as he took a seat. "Oh my dear god! Not Ricky! He's my pop's pride and joy . . . and now . . . he's gone from drugs?"

"I know what this news means to you. Son, as much as we want to keep a fine soldier as yourself, your parents need you now. Pack your things. I'll arrange for the next flight to take you home."

"Thank you, sir. I appreciate that."

A short time later in the army transit barracks, JP packed his belongings into a black steamer trunk. He placed some cash and several not-yet mailed letters in a larger envelope along with another packet of rubber-banded opened and already-read love letters. He closed and locked his trunk. Soon, the trunk was carried off by some fellow soldiers who loaded it on a bus bound for the airport.

Tokyo International Airport
A Short Time Later

After waiting nearly two hours in the crowded airport terminal at night, JP boarded a military 707 bound for the States. At this point, he felt comfortable that once he was home and everything got settled concerning his brother, he'll claim he and his late brother's inheritance from Professor Henry Prestol. He'll travel to Harrisburg and simply withdraw his brother's share of the money from Henry's Mercantile Bank account. "There's got to be millions in that account to date because of Henry's handling of the colonel's research money along with Ricky's drug sales, and Henry's late brother's money from the South Vietnamese officials for his recovered artifacts."

Meanwhile inside the international cargo hangar at the Tokyo airport, Sergeant JP Sheridan's black steamer trunk was accidently loaded onto another flight. Above hangs a sign the read "Hong Kong."

Kyle, in the attic of his grandparents' home, forcefully broke the lock off of his late daddy's steamer trunk. He and Jen began to examine the trunk's contexts. Inside were his late father's army uniforms, war medals and ribbons, a ceremonial sword, and several unopened envelopes addressed to Ricky, Professor Prestol, and Suzanne Hardesty. Kyle opened the first envelope that was addressed to his grandparents. He gently lifted the typed letter out of the envelope and unfolded it. After finding better light near the turret window, he began to read out loud. Jen listened intently.

7 OCTOBER 1970, VIETNAM

Dear Mom and Dad,

Greetings! Captain David Prestol led me and our platoon on another daring nighttime mission—the seventh this month. Each time, I and my buddies risk life and limb, the captain always brings back many souvenirs of the occasion. On these covert missions into Cambodia, we recover stolen art and artifacts that once belonged to the Vietnamese State Museum in Saigon. The gold statues and rare jade and gems, I found out, all have a handsome reward attached. Captain Prestol has amassed several million dollars through negotiations with the corrupt South Vietnamese government. Money has been sent to his brother, chemistry professor Henry Prestol at Farnsworth College. Captain David tells me that his brother has a Mercantile account in Harrisburg.

Whenever our platoon moves, I am called upon to personally guard the captain's valuables. I'll write again soon.

Your loving son, JP

"That letter from your late daddy did explain a lot about his involvement with Henry Prestol's brother," said Jen.

"Get a load of this!" he told her as he removed two thousand dollars in cash from the envelope."

"Isn't that a wonderful gift!" she exclaimed with joy.

"Jen, there's lots of opened letters in here."

Kyle's hands began to tremble as he unfolded another letter with handwriting on one side and numbers scribbled all over the reverse side.

"Here, Jen. Please read this to me. It's addressed to my mom. I think this is real important to our future together."

"Of course, let's sit here on the floor together."

As she began to read to him, he closed his eyes and tried to visualize his deceased daddy writing this letter.

21 OCTOBER, 1970
Vietnam

To my unborn heir,

During the past twelve months I have gone on many covert missions. Our platoon alone has inflicted major damage to the enemy—the North Vietnamese who are called the Viet Cong. Each of our missions resulted in some sort of setback for them. But during each mission, my commanding officer, Capt. David Prestol, U.S. Army, had personally taken an interest in recovering objects of art or jewelry from these mission locations. The captain has an older brother named Henry Prestol. He is on the teaching staff at Farnsworth College.

There is some type of arrangement between the college and the nearby army medical research facility, Fort Douglas. Since I work closely with the captain, he and his brother have made me a partner. We are sending money from the sale of these artifacts and gems to Henry Prestol at Farnsworth College. He's using the funds to personally buy a chemical company that will manufacturer a new version of phencyclidine that they call Sernyl. The military has a strong interest in obtaining his modified drug formula for research purposes and pays top dollars. A lot of money has been deposited into a local bank account. I have coded the account number, which Professor Prestol gave me, on the back of this note. You are listed as Kyle and/or Kathleen Sheridan as one of the heirs to this account should anything ever happen to Captain David Prestol, Professor Henry Prestol, or me.

Love,
Daddy

Jen, with sympathetic eyes, glanced up from the letter at her emotionally drained boyfriend. Kyle, with tears running down his face, was holding an old photograph of his father and sobbed,

"Daddy, I miss you so much. I will always honor your memory. Thank you, Daddy, for your concern about me."

"Kyle, I love you so much," she said as she gently embraced and kissed him. "I think your daddy would approve of everything we're doing. Come, close the trunk and let's go downstairs for a breath of fresh air."

Kyle and Jen returned all the contents to the trunk, closed the lid, and left it unlocked. Together, they tightly held each other's hands and departed for home.

As twilight faded that Thursday evening, Kyle and Jen saw a white car with black glass windows quickly leave the parking lot of their apartment building as they approached. Jen screamed as the white car sped directly for them. "They're heading right for us!"

Kyle yelled out, "Move over! You sons of bitches!"

The two cars nearly sideswiped each other as the white car sped off. Kyle, visibly shaken from the ordeal, pulled into his parking space and said, "Who were those crazy bastards?"

"I . . . I've never seen that car around here before," replied an upset Jen. "Come on. Let's get inside."

The young couple's apartment door had been forced open. They cautiously entered into their darkened apartment. Every item in their apartment had been torn or cut open and dumped on the floor. Jen, in utter disbelief, cried, "Oh god! No! They've ruined everything!"

Kyle held her and hung his head, saying, "Oh Jen! I'm so sorry it has come down to this."

They entered, reclosed and locked the apartment door, and surveyed the damage. Together they moved through the living room, bedroom, and into the kitchen.

"Can you tell if anything's missing?" he asked her.

"All the files are gone, and here . . . read this," she said while handing him what appeared to be a ransom note.

Kyle, with trembling hands read the note out loud.

Kyle Sheridan!

Your grandparents are in protective custody with me in my private laboratory. You have 48 hours to turn over Master Sergeant John P. Sheridan's Mercantile Bank account funds to me or you will never see Richard, Sr., and Mary alive again.

Travis Cummings, M.D.

"Oh, Kyle! I'm so scared now," pleaded Jen.

"Grab some clothes, and let's get the hell away from here."

Within the past week, both Kyle's and Jen's world that was full of hope and promise had been turned upside down. Fears and threats of harm have now confronted both of them. Paranoia set in as they each felt their every move was being monitored. Everyone they knew now became someone who might report on their whereabouts and turn them in. With his grandparents' lives in jeopardy and their personal possessions ruined, the couple sought refuge back at the grandparents' home in Gettysburg.

Lying in the antique poster bed, Kyle's mind reeled with all that had recently happened. "Oh Jen, I had no idea those files would get us in this kind of trouble. I'm really sorry."

"Well, I'm the one who wanted to know this stuff too."

"What should we do next?"

"First thing tomorrow, we must go back to our bank and deposit the cash we have from your daddy's trunk. Then we'll return to Farnsworth College and try to find out something about Dr. William Gray. I think he's our best hope."

"Sounds good, my love."

"We'll return to campus using Grandpa's car to turn in our assignments and then try finding someone who might know the whereabouts of Dr. Gray."

"I just hope and pray your grandparents are okay."

"Yeah, me too. If that old fucking Dr. Cummings harms them . . . he'll pay dearly. Good night, Jen. I love you."

"I love you too. Good night."

"I'm going downstairs for a little while. You go ahead and fall sleep. I'm not tired at the moment."

He left the bedroom and closed the door. He proceeded up to the attic to recover his daddy's opened letters from the steamer trunk.

Once he entered the kitchen, he placed the letters on the table. After fixing a meatloaf sandwich, he began to read each letter. Most of the correspondence was between his daddy and his future wife who was then his girlfriend from high school, Suzanne Hardesty. However,

Kyle's eyes opened wide as he began to read another love letter between his daddy and Melanie Dulane concerning their renewed love for one another. Kyle was shocked to learn that Melanie was apparently more in love with JP than with Ricky, her live-in boyfriend and supposedly father of Jennifer. Kyle sat and stared at the phrase,

"Once Ricky is gone, taken out by the colonel, you'll be mine forever!"

Feeling tired and confused, he returned upstairs and snuggled against his sleeping Jennifer.

26

Day Ten
Friday
September 23, 1994

Following their visit to the Clemetsburg Bank and Trust where Kyle deposited the two thousand dollars into their checking account, he and Jen then drove the short distance to Farnsworth's campus.

Friday morning's fog shrouded the campus again as Kyle parked his car in the lot. After they had finished breakfast and coffee in the student union, they attend Professor Moore's 10:00 a.m. class. Just prior to the start of class, Professor Moore spotted through a window Kyle and Jen coming into the building. She quickly placed a call from her upstairs office.

"Hello, campus police. This is Professor Sheila Moore. The prime suspects have arrived for my ten-o'clock class."

"Excellent, Professor Moore, I'll relay the message to Dr. Cummings that the Sheridan boy and his girlfriend are in your class. Act normal. Don't allow them to suspect anything's up. Goodbye."

Fifty minutes later, the hall bell rang on the ground floor of the engineering building. Students walked out from Professor Moore's classroom into the fluorescent-lighted corridor.

"I'm going to find Professor Hill," Kyle told Jen.

"I'm going back to the library archives and see if I can find anything on the whereabouts of Dr. Gray."

"For God's sake, please be careful."

They quickly kissed and then walked in separate directions out through the double doors. Kyle did not notice any campus police anywhere.

Jennifer entered the library and quickly passed the front desk. The clerk on duty glanced over from his computer screen and watched as Jen entered the elevator for the lower level. He reached for the phone and after dialing the number said, "She's inside and heading for the archives again. Sure. No problem."

Jennifer casually stepped off the elevator and found an open cubby to put her purse. The area appeared deserted. She took a seat in front of a nearby microfiche machine. Her concentration was focused on more newspaper clippings about the campus unrest in 1971. Pictures of Ricky Sheridan and Teddy Lancer appeared. Nothing could be located on psychology professor William Gray.

Suddenly, two military-style campus police approached her from behind. One had a hypodermic needle and quickly injected her in the neck. She immediately collapsed into his arms. Together the men carried her back through a service entrance to a waiting car. She was laid across the rear seat of the white car with the black windows. She remained unconscious as the car sped toward an unknown location.

At the same time, across the street in the political science building, Kyle sat across from Professor Hill who was seated at his desk.

"This has really been one hell of a week for me, Professor."

"Why's that, Mr. Sheridan? The semester's just started."

"Well, Professor, my girlfriend, Jennifer Howser, has persuaded me to help her. We've spent a lot of time recently trying to locate her diseased birthparents who once attended college here in the late '60s and early '70s."

"That can be very difficult, especially without good leads."

"She's had some success in the campus library archives and indicated to me that a former psychology professor from here named Dr. William Gray might be a big help to her."

"That's a name I haven't heard round these parts for quite some time."

"I was wondering if you ever knew of him."

"Yes, I did. Probably, about ten years ago, I needed to talk to him about some of the bizarre event happening around here in the mid-eighties. He's the guy that was fired after blowing the whistle to the FBI about our female dean back in '72. I still think that's why she hung herself from her barn rafters."

Kyle replied to Professor Hill, "I've only recently heard about Ms. Alexander's suicide."

"It certainly was ironic that she died just as Watergate broke and the FBI boys ran back to D.C., leaving our beloved institution alone."

"Do you think Dr. Gray would still be alive?"

"Probably so because he used to be a health guru. You know, weight training and exercise fanatic."

"Do you have any idea where Jen and I might find him?"

"As I recall, he had a private practice somewhere in the Washington, D.C., area awhile back. Maybe he's still there."

"Thanks, Professor. I'm heading over to the library now to tell her. She'll be pleased. See you later."

"Tell her if you all ever find Bill Gray, that he's still not welcome here on this campus. Good day, Kyle."

Once Kyle left and the door was closed, Professor Hill made a phone call. "Hello. This is Hill. May I speak to Dr. Cummings?"

"What is it, Professor?"

"Young Mr. Sheridan just paid me a visit. It seems he and his girlfriend need to find Bill Gray now."

"Well, well. I'll be damned. It looks like we're in for a reunion of sorts. I'll notify the others. Thanks."

Kyle crossed the street and entered Farnsworth's brand-new library. "Excuse me, Jerry. Do you know where I might find Jennifer?"

"She took the elevator downstairs a little while ago and hasn't come back up."

"Thanks, buddy."

Kyle took the elevator downstairs, and a sense of uneasiness overcame him immediately once he entered the deserted-looking archive room.

"Jen, Jen, where are you? Come on. We have to get on back. Jen!"

He panicked when he could not find her. After recovering her purse in the cubby, he noticed and picked up the empty hypodermic needle lying on the floor. He cried out, "Oh my god, no! No! No!"

Kyle ran up the stairs, clutching her purse and entered one of the phone booths just inside the lobby.

"Hello, Washington, D.C., information? Yes, may I have the number of Dr. William Gray? Thanks."

He scribbled down the number and then dialed. "Come on. Come on. Hello. Dr. Gray? Damn, answering machine . . . Yes. Hello, Dr. Gray. My name is Kyle Sheridan. I'm the twenty-four-year-old son of the late John and Suzanne Sheridan. I need to talk with you immediately over a very urgent matter . . . I have less than forty-eight hours to come up with ransom demands made by a Dr. Travis Cummings regarding stolen money or something. The ransom note states that people I love will be hurt. Call me later at the home of Richard Sheridan, Sr., in Gettysburg. Thanks, Dr. Gray. Please help me if you can."

Visibly shaken, Kyle hung up the receiver and tried to calm himself a bit with some deep breaths. Feeling somewhat better, he walked past Jerry at the desk and said, "She must have gone out the other exit. Catch you later."

Kyle left the library still carrying Jen's purse. He also had his other textbooks under his arm. He pulled the bill of his baseball hat down low to cover his face as he noticed a campus police car approaching. The car passed him without incident as he hurriedly unlocked and opened the door to his grandpa's late-model Oldsmobile Cutlass. Starting the car, he then drove off campus.

Thursday's lunchtime found Kyle back at his empty grandparents' house in the kitchen alone, fixing a sandwich. The phone rang.

"Sheridan residence, may I help you?"

A reassuring mature voice on the other end said, "Kyle Sheridan please. This is Dr. William Gray returning his call."

"Oh, Dr. Gray! Thanks, man, for calling me back."

"Son, you're message sounded so urgent. I think I've a good idea what's wrong."

"Sir, I'm currently a grad student at Farnsworth College and recently discovered some 'Top Secret' files in Professor Roger Hill's office."

"Kyle, before you go any further, you must know the behind-the-scenes operation at that campus."

"Dr. Gray, it seems like everyone's nerve was plucked when I started asking questions around here."

"For nearly twenty years now, weird things have been happening at that college."

"I believe that Dr. Travis Cummings, MD, is the cause."

"He is. He recently completed serving twenty years in a federal prison for extortion, money laundering, and theft of government funds. He's extremely dangerous."

"Sir, his people, I believe, kidnapped my fiancée and my grandparents. They are being held at some secret research facility, and he is holding them until I withdraw money from some damn secret bank account that my late father was part of. Dr. Gray, I really could use a hand. I just don't know where else to turn."

"Kyle, I remember promising your grandparents I'd watch out for you. That's something I've regretted not doing until now. Come, drive down to my Georgetown address this afternoon, and we'll plan our strategy."

"Dr. Gray, there are so many questions and so little time. I'll leave shortly. See you in a few hours. Thanks again. Goodbye.

27

A sign over the door read "Patient Care." Dr. William Gray entered the room. His new patient, Melanie Dulane, was seated, restrained in her chair and sleeping. She had been under his treatment for the past two years.

"Hello, Melanie. How are you?"

Raising her head, she said, "Oh, it's you."

"I have reviewed your many files again, Melanie. I continue to find you're still living out your troubling past. How would you describe today your life before coming here?"

"Oh, Dr. Gray, it's so hard to think differently with so much hatred inside of me."

"Melanie, you're as lovely as the first day we met."

"Yes, I remember. It was like yesterday. Oh, Dr. Gray. Will I ever get over Ricky and his brother, JP? They both did me so wrong."

"Don't get yourself so upset over the past. Look toward a new beginning."

Melanie began to cry, saying, "That's easy for you to say. But I'm the one sentenced to relive my mistakes. Ricky's dead, and JP is somewhere out there living the good life. I don't even know who adopted and are raising my own precious daughter, Jennifer."

"Now don't get upset. I'm positive she's growing up in a loving family setting."

"If only JP hadn't changed all that!"

"After all this time, you really dislike this fellow P."

Melanie began to shout hysterically and pushed at her restraints. She yelled, "It's his fault! It's his fucking fault! JP gave his own brother those tainted drugs. I know he did. He hated his own brother, my lover, Ricky. And I was the one convicted of Ricky Sheridan's death. It's not fair! Not fair!"

White-coated men quickly entered the room and held Melanie as Dr. Gray administered an injection. Soon she fell back into a deep sleep once again.

"That was close, Dr. Gray. She's really not responding very well to her treatment. I recommend changing her daily medication," commented an administrator standing in the doorway.

"I will, sir, following Melanie's latest outburst. She's simply a burned-out acid eater. That's all. Someday, her will to fight will change."

"I hope you're there when she does," replied the administrator.

Three Months Later
April 29, 1976

Inside the hospital ward late one moonless night, twenty-five-year-old Melanie Dulane overpowered her female attendant and choked the older woman to death. After removing the attendant's clothes and putting them on, Melanie quickly escaped out a window into the darkness. She carried the attendant's purse, money, and ID.

Tudor Apartments
Dupont Circle, Washington, D.C.
April 30, 1976

The elevator doors opened and Melanie Dulane glanced at the numbers on the wall plaque. Apartment 8-C was on her left around the first corner.

Picking up her satchel, she casually approached the door and lightly knocked.

The door slowly opened on to a security chain. Old girlfriend, Kiki Flaund, welcomed her visitor.

"Melanie! Thank God you made it."

"Well, aren't you going to open your door?"

Once the door was unchained, Kiki hugged Melanie. "I can't believe it's really you. You look so different with short hair."

"Yes, it's been a long time, and I really appreciate your invitation to let me stay for a while."

The two girlfriends entered the apartment. Melanie placed her satchel and a multicolored umbrella near the closet door.

Melanie glanced back and forth and commented, "Your place is wonderful."

"I really love living here. It's close to everything. A new Metro station is being built across the street, and at night this place really jumps."

"I passed several interesting-looking restaurants and bars getting over here," Melanie told her friend.

"My favorite is the cafe down on the corner of M and Connecticut Avenue.

Their food is fabulous but slightly expensive, so I only go there for special occasions like now!" She giggled.

Melanie gave Kiki another hug and whispered, "Oh, Kiki, you're such a good friend."

Together the girls took a seat on the sofa.

"This opens into your bed, Melanie. My other guests said it's pretty comfortable."

"I'm sure it'll be fine compared to that hospital bed I had."

"Imagine so. Can you tell me anything about your living there?"

"It was sort of quiet and peaceful compared with the hectic and loud music and those bright lights we were accustomed to back in the early '70s."

"Has it really been three years ago that you went away?"

Melanie began to sob and said, "Suppose so. I . . . don't know . . ."

"There, there. You're safe here. There shouldn't be any problems now. Forget the past. Your world will soon become full again with new and wonderful things."

"I . . . I sure hope so."

Kiki left Melanie on the sofa. In a little while, she returned with two cups of tea. Handing one cup to Melanie, she said, "I hope this makes you feel better, stranger."

"Oh, Kiki! This is just what I needed."

"Things have really changed in three years, Melanie."

"I realize that. I need to play catch-up."

"What do you honestly want to do with your life now?"

"I just don't know. I started many things back then, especially with my man, Ricky Sheridan."

"Oh, Melanie! Will you ever let him go?"

"Probably not, when he died, my world collapsed into a million pieces.

Nothing seems to fit together anymore . . . and Ricky's younger brother, JP, is totally to blame."

"That whole mess was such a shame."

"I'm going to ruin his world the same way he's done mine."

"Now, how will you be able to do that?" Kiki asked.

"I'll get to him through his wife."

"Joey wants me to marry him in the worse way."

"Aren't you?"

"Not yet. He's so involved in President Ford's reelection campaign that he spends no time with me at all," she lamented.

"Didn't you expect that?" Melanie asked.

With malice in her voice, she yelled, "No, damn it! I expected him to remain in law school like a good little lawyer-to-be should."

"Oh, Kiki, your vision of the future seems as uncertain as mine."

Just then, the wall clock chimed six times. Kiki told her friend, "Come on.

It's time for dinner."

"Kiki, please don't take me to that cafe tonight. I have neither nice clothes nor any money."

"Nonsense, girl! Get yourself into my closet and grab an outfit. We're using Joey's new credit card tonight!"

Shortly thereafter, the girls were seated near the picture window with a full view of the bustling corner. People, cars, and buses continued to pass during their meal.

"Kiki! I've needed this change."

"I agree."

"I just feel it's important for me personally to build my life again completely fresh."

"And how are you going to do it, girlfriend?"

Thinking to herself and then remembering how she had overpowered the nurse and stole her identity, Melanie told Kiki, "Before I came by this afternoon, I went through Woodie's Department Store and stood near the counter where ladies were filling out credit applications. I was able to remember one in particular and copied her address and driver's license number."

"But what can that do?" asked Kiki.

Continuing to lie, Melanie said, "I just walked into the district's Motor Vehicle office, told them I had lost my license, paid the three dollars, and got this new fancy driver's license," she said while proudly displaying her new license.

"My god! Melinda Savage you are!" Kiki brought her hands toward her mouth in utter disbelief.

"Yes, sweetie pie, and soon, with your help and your boyfriend's credit card, I'll open a checking account at that new Chevy Chase Bank on Dupont Circle."

"Don't lose that thought. It's good."

Following dinner, the reunited girlfriends went for a walk in the chilly evening. Soon they entered a disco lounge featuring an extended happy hour and ladies' night specials. No sooner had they seated themselves when two handsome professional bachelor types approached and asked the girls to dance.

Soon the entire dance floor came alive. It contained multicolored lights under the floor, which blinked to the loud thumping music. Each dancer was clad in polyester bell bottoms and either platform or spiked heels. This jet-setter crowd jammed fast and furious to the latest Donna Summer and Village People hits.

After returning back to the apartment around eleven, Kiki turned on the bedroom TV before retiring. Melanie was in the living room and had gotten settled comfortably on the sofa bed. The evening had been both exciting and tiring for Melanie.

The past four years of confinement at Lebanon State Mental Hospital between 1972 and 1976 had been quiet and sedative. Now Melanie threw herself back to the world of reality. Could she adjust or tune out? That was something she pondered in her mind as she lay on the sofa bed. She heard sirens, people talking on the television, colored neon lights flashing beyond her window. None of these was permitted during her years of treatment.

"Is this all a dream? Did I actually kill that bitch nurse with my bare hands and escape from that hospital? Am I now really free to pursue my dreams of revenge on JP Sheridan?" Melanie silently thought as she tried to fall asleep.

Preparing for bed herself, Kiki casually glanced at the TV and noticed a reporter in Philadelphia talking to a young male artist. The interviewed artist was explaining his recent appointment by the Bicentennial Commission to paint a series of presidential portraits to be displayed onboard the Freedom Train.

Kiki recognized the man immediately and became excited. She called to Melanie, "It's JP Sheridan, Melanie. He's on the fucking news!"

"What?" sleepy-eyed Melanie exclaimed. "Where is he?"

"He's being interviewed in Philadelphia. Seems he's involved in this year's big bicentennial celebration."

"Oh, Kiki! That's wonderful news," replied Melanie with her mind reeling of revenge.

"I'm off tomorrow, so why don't we go there together for the day? You can meet JP, and then we'll go shopping at Wannamakers."

"Oh, could we?" her newly found girlfriend pleaded.

"No problem. I'll simply charge our train tickets on Joey's credit card."

"That's such a nice thing to do for me."

"On the other hand, do you think it is a wise thing to do so soon after getting out of the hospital?" asked Kiki.

Melanie looked like she was in a trance. "He'll be surprised when we meet again." She smiled and sat on the edge of Kiki's bed. "You know, Kiki, I'm going to do something really different this time. I'm turning on the charm."

"You screamed real loud at him three years ago during your trial," Kiki reminded her guest.

"Well, I'll be nicer this time. I'm going to rebuild our friendship. And besides, he reminds me so much of Ricky. Young, strong, focused, and full of life. Did I mention he's great in bed too?" She giggled.

"Oh, Melanie, your treatments have made you a changed woman. I'm so glad."

"Thanks again for a terrific evening. That disco lounge was just the party scene I needed. Would I be asking too much if I we could get high tonight?"

"Well, I know it's getting late. But since I'm off tomorrow, it'll be all right.

Come into the kitchen."

Kiki slipped on her satin robe and fuzzy slippers and took her guest by the hand. The young women walked through the darkened apartment and entered the kitchen. Melanie sat down, and Kiki opened a cabinet and took out a canister. "This pot came from Mexico and is quite nice."

Kiki rolled a joint and then turned on the radio to an alternative pop station. Selections of Janis Joplin and then Iron Butterfly quickly filled the small room along with the aroma of the pot. The girls took turns passing the lighted joint back and forth. The mind-numbing sensation and the music helped Melanie relax. The past twenty-four hours since her escape from the state hospital compound had been a whirlwind ride. Now, finally, Melanie felt at peace and safe with Kiki.

With dilated pupils and soft-spoken words, both girls said their good nights.

"Kiki, you're such a wonderful friend."

"Good night, Melanie. Sleep well. We'll talk in the morning.

28

The alarm clock went off at 8:00 a.m. Kiki arose and walked through the living room toward the kitchen. As she passed her sleeping girlfriend on the sofa bed, she noticed several scars on Melanie's wrists. Last night, the long-sleeved polyester outfit she wore did not let those scars show. Kiki felt sympathy toward Melanie. Her world of drugs, sex, and treatments had certainly taken a toll.

At twenty-five, both girls had similar experiences. Kiki's life was once again much better. She was now engaged to Farnsworth graduate, class of 1972, Joey Henson. He overflowed with definite political aspirations.

"We graduated together, have been happily in love, employed, and furnished this apartment," she thought as she put water on to boil for coffee.

"Poor Melanie's has done none of this."

Kiki sat down at the table, staring at the marijuana roach lying in the ashtray. "Her life's like that," she thought. "All rolled up, lighted, inhaled, and then extinguished. But how nice was the experience."

Just then the phone rang.

"Good morning, Joey. How are President Ford and Chicago doing this morning?" Kiki asked, excited to hear her man's voice again. "Yes, Melanie arrived last night, and we went out for dinner and some disco. She seemed to have really enjoyed herself."

"What's on your agenda today since you're off work?" he asked.

"Melanie and I are heading up to Philadelphia this morning to find her old boyfriend and do some shopping. The train should return around 148 9:00 p.m. Can you meet us, and we'll do dinner there at Union Station on Chinatown?"

"That sounds fine to me. But I can't promise at this point."

"Why not?" she asked with a frown.

"President Ford is meeting all of us late this afternoon at the White House for a strategy meeting on his reelection. There seems to be this peanut farmer from Georgia who's ahead in the primaries. We've got to make some changes if the Republicans are going to win in November."

"I'll call your office tonight when Melanie and I get to Union Station."

"Do that, darling. I've got to run. Love you."

"It's only 7:00 a.m. and you're on Central Time! Run to what?"

Kiki heard the phone click, and then she hung up her phone. Her hands began to tremble, so she reached for the canister and rolled another joint. After pouring herself a cup of coffee, she lit the toke. She sighed as her attention was again drawn to the other butt in the ashtray. Inhaling, she sleighed,

"Sometimes I feel as alone as you do, Melanie."

Union Station
Washington, D.C.
May 1, 1976

Kiki and Melanie left their taxi and walked past several burly construction workers in their early twenties, scurrying about near the entrance of Union Station. "Once this Metro stop is completed, you'll be able to get from Georgetown to here in ten minutes."

"That'll be nice." Melanie smiled as she eyed the men. "My, would you get a load of that redhead with a beard and hard hat. He's gorgeous."

"He reminds me of the guy from the Village People."

"I'd like to trip out with him sometime."

"I'm sure you would. This way, Melanie, he's busy."

The girls purchased their roundtrip ticket and followed the crowd toward the track level. "The train's here. Good. Hurry, they're announcing departure in three minutes."

Stepping up to the platform, they were welcomed aboard by another handsome young Amtrak conductor.

"He can punch my ticket anytime," whispered Melanie to her giggling girlfriend.

They were able to sit together on the crowded train.

The few hours on the train were pleasant and passed quickly. Upon arriving at the Thirtieth Street Station, the girls rode the escalators to the street level and grabbed the first taxi they saw.

"Where to, ladies?" asked the seemingly friendly native.

"The Bicentennial Commission Headquarters please," requested Melanie.

"Sure. It's not far from here," replied the cab driver as they quickly sped away from the curbside.

"Where are you ladies from?"

"Washington, D.C.," they replied.

"Just here for the day to do a little business and a lot of shopping," added Kiki.

The cab covered about twenty blocks before coming to a screeching halt in front of a somewhat dilapidated-looking warehouse in a less-than-desirable section of the downtown. The two girls looked at each other and shrugged their shoulders.

"That'll be three dollars and fifty cents."

Kiki handed the man a five-dollar bill. She opened the cab door and got out. As the taxi left, they could see the street was somewhat deserted. In the distance, they saw the cupola of Independence Hall. The sign on the door indicated that this actually was their intended destination.

Upon entering the building, Melanie and Kiki felt somewhat relieved at the sight of a receptionist on the phone, sitting at a desk in the dimly lighted lobby. On her desk was a miniature display of the thirteen original colonies' flags. Her nameplate said, "Ms. G. Thomas."

When she hung up the phone, she greeted the two women.

Melanie stepped forward and said, "Good morning, I'm Ms. Dulane, and this is my friend, Ms. Flaund. Last night, on the 11:00 p.m. news, we watched a reporter interviewing a Mr. John Paul Sheridan about his art commissions for this year's celebration. Is he here?"

"Yes, Mr. Sheridan should be taking a lunch break shortly from his meeting upstairs. He'll probably come down here and leave for lunch. May I call upstairs and tell him you're here?"

"That'll be fine." Melanie smiled.

"You ladies may wait over there."

As the girls seated themselves, they couldn't help notice several large paintings on the walls that depicted famous colonial Americans' portraits. All the art had "JP Sheridan '75" in the lower right-hand corners.

"Your ex-boyfriend is quiet an excellent artist," whispered Kiki.

"I never knew he could paint that good. Honest."

When the elevator door opened, Melanie and Kiki stood up. Twenty-five-year-old JP Sheridan, wearing a light blue leisure suit, platform shoes, and sideburns, was immediately recognized by Melanie among the passengers departing the car.

"JP!"

"Melanie? Is that really you?" he responded with both shock and delight.

"Oh yes," she said, taking hold of his hand. "I'm truly sorry about the past, and I'm trying to build a new life."

"Man, you really surprised me. I thought you were still under Dr. Gray's care."

"He left the hospital about six weeks ago to begin his own practice. I was released the other day all better!"

"I see. And who's this lovely creature?"

Blushing somewhat, Kiki was introduced by Melanie as her Farnsworth College roommate. "May we join you for lunch?"

"Certainly, I go to this little deli a couple of blocks from here, and their corned beef's excellent."

JP led the way, and shortly, the three were seated in a booth inside the bustling deli. After ordering, he asked, "How did you ever find me here?"

"We saw you being interviewed on the news last night," said Kiki.

"Oh, JP, can you and I begin to build a new life together?" pleaded Melanie.

"Yeah! Right on, sister!" he seemingly mocked her. "Melanie, I've married Suzanne, and we have a young son named Kyle. We live in a nice house in Rose Hill Manor, and my life's pretty settled."

Nearly in tears, Melanie lowered her head and quietly asked, "Do you love her?"

JP's response was delayed, knowing what he said could be the chance he needed to leave Suzanne and Kyle. He could then run free with Melanie and her drugged-up friends and become the totally abstract artist he yearned to be.

The party life could begin again with her for sure.

"The attraction has gone away. I'm ready for a change."

"Oh, JP! I love you so much. Please let me into your world."

Kiki's eyes widened, and her jaw fell like a ton of bricks just hit her. She could not believe her ears. This woman who was apparently consumed with a hatred of this man now said she was in love with him!

"Melanie! Do you know what you just said?" asked Kiki.

"Yes, girlfriend, and together with JP, my life will be normal and wonderful again."

"Eat your sandwich, girl."

"JP, I'm only in town for a few hours today, and Kiki wanted to go shopping."

He scribbled an address and phone number on a napkin and handed it to Melanie. "It's my studio number in Georgetown. I'm going back tomorrow.

Call me there, and we'll meet."

He and Melanie then began a long embrace. Kiki said nothing and continued eating her sandwich wide-eyed after Melanie blinked one eye during the kiss. After lunch, the girls said goodbye to JP and hailed another cab for Wannamaker's Department Store.

May 2, 1976

The following afternoon was rainy. Melanie stood on the corner of Twentieth and Connecticut Avenue holding her multicolored umbrella.

Around two, she saw JP approach in his new silver '76 Datsun 260ZX. He pulled curbside, and she quickly got in.

"Hello again, JP!"

"How are you, Melanie?"

"I'm fine today. The train trip last night was so relaxing that I slept the entire way to back to D.C."

As they drove off, he asked, "Is Kiki's apartment near here?"

"Yes, right off of DuPont Circle. Her place is cute and has a wonderful view of Rock Creek Park and M Street."

"Melanie, there's one question that's been nagging me since yesterday?"

"What's that?"

"The last time we met was at the trial over three years ago, and you tried very hard to implicate me in Ricky's overdose. Why?"

"Your brother, Ricky, had become extremely desponded and depressed in the fall of 1971 after being accused of double crossing the colonel and Professor Prestol. Army colonel Dr. Travis Cummings had told Ricky and me that you and Henry Prestol's brother, David, in Vietnam were all working together dealing in coke and heroin."

"That's a damn lie!"

"Please let me continue," begged Melanie.

Calming down a bit, he said, "Go ahead."

"Army doctor Cummings then worked closely with Ricky until November '71 when Ricky suddenly became so sick and then he died."

"But I never sent Ricky or the doctor any drugs from Vietnam," explained JP. "We only sent cash. Captain David Prestol was my platoon leader, and we were involved in recovering stolen art objects for the Vietnamese State Museum in Saigon. We sent the reward money to Henry Prestol who had supposedly opened a secret bank account that no one knows the whereabouts of since his mysterious disappearing act."

"The dean of Farnsworth College, Tricia Alexander committed suicide in June 1972, and Professor Henry Prestol vanished. Not even that Dr. Cummings had a clue where the money was," replied Melanie. "So you never sent your brother any drugs?"

"Not an ounce of anything. I swear it."

"Oh my! Then how did Ricky really die?"

"Hmmmm. I'd bet all the money in that missing account that Colonel Cummings arranged for Ricky's death because he was no longer needed . . . and probably knew too damn much about his secret medical research project.

Well, here we are."

"This is your studio?" she asked, eyeing the seemingly vacant building.

"The door's on the side, and I use the second-floor loft area. Come on.

I'll show you."

He and Melanie entered his studio area, and she was surprised at the many finished and unfinished canvases that were placed about on easels. "Oh, JP! These paintings are simply beautiful."

"The plans call for these presidential portraits to be on display aboard the Freedom Train."

"Yes, I remember that from your TV interview." Then she commented,

"And these others?"

"Several go to the U.S. Postal Service for stamp designs, and this one will be sent to France for their ceremony."

"Oh, JP, you really are making a mark for yourself. I'm so pleased for you."

"Melanie, come over here. Let's sit down and talk about our future together."

"Does you wife, Suzanne, support and appreciate your art?"

"I think she's somewhat jealous. But she has her own modeling career and is quite successful in her own right."

"Well, you're very talented, and she should have developed a real appreciation for your work. I have in only ten minutes."

"Thank you, Melanie. You're most kind. But right now there seems to be no way I could convince Suzanne that I want her to leave or me to move out."

"JP, come close to me and listen. I know a way."

"But how?"

"Together, we can mess with her mind. Perhaps over the next several weeks or so to the point where she'll feel she needs to visit a shrink."

"Hmmmm. Go on."

"I'll reestablish old connections, and you can feed her. You and I can slowly drive her over the edge and possibly even get her committed to a mental hospital somewhere. LSD will do that."

"That doesn't sound too difficult. She's already very hyper and under a lot of pressure in her line of work."

"Are your parents still around?"

"Sure. And they wouldn't mind watching little Kyle sometimes when we play games with Suzanne's head. Oh, Melanie, what a damn good plan!"

Melanie eased herself closer, and they began to passionately kiss. Soon, their clothes were strewn on the studio's floor and JP was rolling some joints for their afternoon delight.

29

Day Eleven
Saturday
September 24, 1994

While driving alone to Dr. Gray's residence in the Georgetown neighborhood of D.C., Kyle passed Rose Hill Manor where he used to live until age five. He now tried and tried to mentally recall some of the disturbing incidents from his childhood past. He could not wait to once again ask Dr. Gray the truth about his parents' lives.

Georgetown Residence
Saturday Evening
September 24, 1994

Dr. Gray paced anxiously through his spacious home, waiting for twenty-four-year-old Kyle to arrive. He had been drinking heavily ever since he and Kyle conversed at lunchtime. He began trying to recall pieces of Kyle's late father and uncle's puzzling life that will enable him to answer many of Kyle's questions. He talked to himself as he wrote on a yellow legal pad. "I was in marriage counseling with Suzanne Sheridan after Melanie Dulane escaped the state hospital and had gotten reacquainted with JP Sheridan."

John P. Sheridan's Residence
Rose Hill Manor
June, 1976

Melanie Dulane was seated once again at the kitchen counter, sipping tea and eating a cookie. Suzanne had left to room and followed five-year-old Kyle down the hallway to the family room.

She settled Kyle in front of the TV and turned on cartoons for him to watch. She left and rechecked to see that Melanie had not moved. She saw Melanie in the kitchen, so she quickly went upstairs to her bedroom.

Suzanne, in a heightened state of fear, dialed the phone and whispered,

"Hello! Dr. Gray, this is Suzanne Sheridan."

"Suzanne, what's the matter?"

"Melanie Dulane is seated in my kitchen right now. Please come over. John's not home, and this woman really frightens me."

"I'm on my way. Don't do anything that would tip her off. She's really a dangerous mental case. Goodbye."

Suzanne regained her composure and left the bedroom. She descended the stairs and checked in on Kyle.

"Mommy, where's daddy's friend?"

"Ms. Melanie was in the kitchen, dear."

"She ain't there no more. Go look."

Suzanne took little Kyle by the hand, and together they left the family room.

"Come, Kyle. Let's take a look."

Suzanne and young Kyle entered the deserted kitchen. Melanie and her multicolored umbrella had vanished. The back door was open. Suzanne looked out into the yard as the rain continued to pour. Just then, they heard the front door bell ring.

Handing Kyle another cookie and closing the back door, she called out,

"Wait a moment. I'm coming!"

Suzanne and young Kyle left the kitchen and hurried seemingly unafraid through the hallway. She turned the door knob slowly while holding Kyle's hand. She called out, "Melanie, is it you?"

The door opened, and her husband was standing on the front porch holding his briefcase. John entered and kissed his trembling wife.

"Hello, darling. Why did you just call the name Melanie?"

Little Kyle pushed his mother back and reached up to his daddy John lifted the boy up for a hug.

Suzanne began sobbing and said, "That woman! Melanie Dulane was just here a little while ago and wanted to meet you."

"Melanie! Here! Where is she?"

She nervously glanced back and forth then said, "She must've left out the back door just a few minutes ago."

Suzanne then glanced into the hall mirror and caught the image of Melanie wielding a kitchen knife. She had emerged from the basement door.

Melanie pushed Suzanne aside and stabbed John in his chest. His face contorted in horror as Suzanne screamed and Kyle was dropped. John's body slumped as Suzanne wrestled Melanie to the floor. Melanie was able to stab Suzanne several times as she screamed.

Young Kyle continued to scream, "Daddy, Daddy!" while pulling on John's raincoat.

Dr. Gray and two district policemen burst into the hallway and confronted Melanie holding a bloody knife.

"Lady! Drop your weapon!"

Melanie screamed, held the bloody knife above her head, and lurched toward the officers. With their weapons drawn, each officer began to immediately open fire. Several of the rounds struck Melanie in the upper torso. She fell backward over the bodies of her victims. Young Kyle, he and his clothes drenched in the blood of his parents and their murderer, was quickly snatched away crying hysterically by the officers and passed into Dr. Gray's waiting arms.

Dr. Gray, continuing to await Kyle's arrival, again thought to himself, "Thank God I arrived in time and rescued little Kyle. I'll never forget that terrible day."

His thoughts were interrupted when he heard a car door slam outside. It was raining hard when Kyle rang the doorbell. When the door opened the door, both men stared at each other for a moment.

Dr. Gray was the youngest looking over-fifty-year-old that Kyle had ever seen. Kyle thought, Old Professor Hill was right. This guy must own his own gym.

Dr. Gray was amazed at how young Kyle resembled his deceased father, JP.

"Thank you for seeing me tonight, sir."

"Kyle Sheridan! My, how you resemble your late father—God rest his soul. Please, come in. Here, I'll take your wet things."

"Thanks, Dr. Gray. As I told you on the phone, my fiancée, Jennifer Howser, and I are graduate students at Farnsworth College. Just this week, many weird things have gone down."

"I heard and read about Dean Henson's murder. That was such a terrible thing."

"His murderer, Teddy Lancer, was just released from jail and returned to get even."

"That sort of behavior was common around Farnsworth's campus a long time ago when I worked there. We all did things and hurt lots of people with seemingly little regret," lamented Bill.

"Sir, both Jen and my grandparents are in protective custody with Dr. Cummings."

"Oh god! No!" Bill responded with a look of panic.

"And I have a lot less than forty-eight hours left to turn over ransom money from some fucking secret bank account," urged Kyle.

"Son, this is very serious. These people are ruthless. Those hostages could be subjected to mind-controlling drugs. You'd better act on this fast and watch yourself very carefully."

"Dr. Gray, that's one of my problems. I have another."

"Are you seeking your past?"

"You may know it better than me."

"Follow me to the study and join me for a drink."

"Thank you. That's just what I need."

Moving into the teak-paneled study full of antiques and rare books on shelves, Dr. Gray poured two drinks and pointed to his desk. Two thick folders had been placed on the edge.

"Since both clients are deceased, I'm at liberty to share this confidential information." He handed Kyle the first folded. "Inside are records of my treatment of Melanie Dulane at Lebanon State Mental following her sentencing on her insanity defense for the drug-overdose death of your uncle, Ricky Sheridan, in November 1972."

30

Upon finishing reading the file on Melanie Dulane, Kyle's eyes were filled with tears. He composed himself to say, "I had no idea about Melanie's involvement other than that terrible day when Daddy and Mommy died, and you, Dr. Gray, were there to help me."

Kyle then opened the second file and glanced wide-eyed. Dr. Gray told him, "This file contained detailed notes of my psychological evaluations and follow-up counseling of your late dear mother, Suzanne. There are notes about Melanie's escape from the hospital, her stalking your father, JP, Suzanne's marital problems with him, Melanie stabbing and killing your parents when you were five years old in 1976, and your custody going to JP's parents."

Kyle now had tears that streamed down his face. They're all here. Aren't they, Dr. Gray?"

"No, Kyle. There's more you probably don't know."

"Can you help me?"

"Yes, I will. This time even I'll settle an old score. Here, take this pistol with you. We may need it."

Finishing his drink, Kyle took a seat in a highbacked leather chair. Dr. Gray told him, "Excuse me for a moment. I need to make a call before we leave. Fix another drink . . . if you want."

"Thanks, but I'm fine."

Kyle watched as Dr. Gray went to his desk and made a phone call. "Hello, this is Dr. William Gray. I need to be connected with the attorney general. She's expecting my return call."

Within a short time, Kyle heard Dr. Gray say, "Yes, Attorney General. It's time we settle a very old score with Dr. Travis Cummings. Everything has been readied. I believe that hostages are being held at Cummings's research facility in Silopanna, Maryland.

"I'm leaving now with young Kyle Sheridan for Farnsworth College to pick up Professor Roger Hill. Then we'll plan to travel to Silopanna. Good night."

Following that conversation, Dr. Gray and Kyle left his office together. They ran through the continuing September rain and got into Kyle's yellow ' 69 Mustang. The car roared off into the night.

"Where'd you ever find a car like this?"

"It used to belong to my late uncle Ricky," replied Kyle proudly.

"This ' 69 Shelby Mustang's a real classic and certainly must be worth a small fortune."

Kyle had to laugh. "Yeah. My buddies get real jealous whenever they see me driving her."

"When your father returned from Vietnam because of your Uncle Ricky's death in November 1971, his belongings never arrived with him. Your mother—God rest her soul—told me once that his steamer trunk contained a Mercantile Bank account number and that you were his unborn named heir. Since the army lost it and both the Prestol brothers died, your father could not evidently access the account."

"Sir, I located the steamer trunk. It's in my grandparent's attic now. Yesterday, I opened it, found an envelope that contained two thousand dollars, and a strange letter saying that account number was on the reverse side. My girlfriend and I checked the number out, and there was no such bank account listed."

"Well, I'll be damned, son. If you ever figure out what those numbers match, there's got to be a bundle of money to claim."

"That sounds good to me. But I'm sort of confused. I was born in 1970 and mother always called me her Hawaiian souvenir. I never knew what that really meant."

"Your mother, Suzanne—God rest her soul—told me then your ex-army father was her high school sweetheart and prom date. After he returned home from Vietnam in November 1971, he attended Farnsworth College while stationed at Fort Douglas during 1972.

After extending his enlistment with the army, he was promoted to master sergeant and given a nice signing-on bonus of several thousand dollars. In early 1973, something happened, and your father went AWOL from the army. He reappeared soon after in the Washington, D.C., metro area and worked there as an itinerant artist. According to your mother, she hired him to do a painting. JP then somehow met her again and her three-year-old son . . . You! They evidently had met years before in Hawaii on New Year's Eve, 1970."

"I suppose I'm the souvenir?"

"When 1972 came to an end, Melanie Dulane had been committed for your uncle Ricky's overdose, Professor Henry Prestol, and his army brother, David, were departed and out of the picture."

"You weren't there either at that time?" asked Kyle.

"I had to leave Farnsworth at the end of May 1972 after threatening to expose the scandalous behavior of Henry Prestol to the FBI."

"How so?"

"Once Colonel Cummings controlled Henry Prestol's mind, he wanted more influence at Farnsworth College."

"Jen and I found old documents about their first female dean, Tricia Alexander. She seemed to have had a zero tolerance for the campus radicals, drugs, and hippies."

"She did until I stumbled on to a lead that took me to an old stone farmhouse near the college. Through a window one night, I watched Henry Prestol get dressed as Tricia Alexander and leave for an evening event at the college."

"What!" exclaimed Kyle in shock and disbelief, "Chemistry professor Henry Prestol and the female dean were the same person!"

"Yeah, isn't that queer!" laughed Dr. Gray. "He was a real cross-dresser. His professor mustache and goatee were all a put-ons."

"Damn! Jen and I found those same items and some sort of map in a metal box under the floorboards of an old abandoned stone farmhouse near Farnsworth College last Saturday while doing research for a class assignment."

"Huh, very interesting," replied Dr. Gray. He then told Kyle, "The army provided all the phony credentials and got him appointed as the college's first female dean! Henry became the puppet that Colonel Travis Cummings needed. His own programmed goons ran both Fort Douglas and Farnsworth College's security program."

"I've just recently met him last week, immediately following Dean Henson's assassination. He's no longer in the army."

"He was just released from the military prison in Fort Leavenworth last month, and he's ready to reclaim the lost fortune that he has always said was rightfully his."

31

Psychologist Dr. William Gray had helped army doctor Colonel Cummings recruit college students and military volunteers from 1969 till June 1972. He was dismissed from the program as an informer to the FBI. He went into protective custody until Cummings was imprisoned in the fall of 1974. Dr. Gray later worked for several years at Lebanon State Mental Hospital where Melanie Dulane was one of his patients. Following that job, he then moved to Georgetown. Since the mid-1980s he had been able to help counsel drug and mentally ill patients.

Bill was never privy to the drug money fund trail that the late Farnsworth chemistry professor Henry Prestol, along with his late brother, army captain David Prestol, had arranged. Bill also knew of the tremendous loss the Sheridan family had experienced. The colonel sacrificed both of their sons, Ricky, Jr., and JP, along with their daughters-in-law, Suzanne Hardesty and Melanie Dulane. Now only JP's son, twenty-two-year-old Kyle Sheridan and his expecting young fiancée, Jennifer Howser, remained alive. They alone could be his key to Cummings's lost fortune.

Kyle told Bill Gray while driving, "Dr. Cummings gave Jen and me instructions not to meddle in the college's internal business."

"Really!" acting coy about recently talking to the doctor himself, he told Kyle, "I had often wondered whatever became of him in prison. So that old bastard must be out by now, and I'm still convinced he created this whole mess just to become famous and rich."

"How so, Dr. Gray?"

"Your good Dr. Cummings, as he calls himself, had paid Farnsworth's chemistry professor Dr. Henry Prestol big government grant bucks in early 1970s to develop a new strain of phencyclidine named Sernyl."

"Yes, my daddy's letter mentioned that. What the hell was it?"

"It was originally called the Peace Pill or PCP. And what's so strange is that old Henry changed the formula to allow for mind conditioning. As crazy as it seems, I believed the doctor programmed Henry to commit suicide after taking the stuff, which allowed Cummings to get all the credit and an army promotion to boot!"

"My fiancée, Jen Howser, is somehow now convinced she's Melanie Dulane's child."

"She very well could be. Melanie's infant daughter was taken from her and given up for adoption at six months old once Melanie was committed following her boyfriend's death, your late uncle Ricky."

"If my uncle Ricky was her father, then we really are first cousins . . . and never could get married!" cried Kyle.

"Ricky Sheridan was not the father of Melanie Dulane's baby daughter."

"You seem to know otherwise," replied Kyle with a feeling of relief.

"You introduce me to your Jennifer, and I'll tell her myself. Come on. Crank these 350 horses. Let's see what this old baby can do."

Kyle accelerated the ' 69 Mustang to over 100 miles per hour in a matter of seconds.

"That's it. That forty-eight-hour ransom note deadline of yours is getting closer," replied Bill Gray.

Around 10:00 p.m., Kyle and Dr. Gray arrived and parked in across the street from the political science building on the Farnsworth College campus. The rain that had fallen most of their trip from Georgetown had subsided. Streetlights reflected on the roadways around the campus. Meanwhile, across the street, a college student-aged guard picked up his phone and called Dr. Cummings. "Excuse me, Doctor. The Sheridan boy and a stranger have just arrived outside and are parked across the street, sir! They've just entered the political science building."

The doctor looked up from a microscope and said, "Excellent. Follow their every move. Don't let them get away."

"Of course not, sir."

"You have orders to arrest them."

"Yes, Doctor. I'll inform the others."

"I want them brought here for conditioning."

The young guard stated, "Sir! Right away, sir!"

At the same time, Kyle unlocked Professor Hill's office. The lights were still on. Together they entered and found the body of Professor Hill slumped over his desk. A handgun was nearby. He had apparently shot himself in the temple.

"Professor Hill! Oh god . . . No!"

"I'm sorry, son . . . We're a little late," responded Dr. Gray, shaking his head in disbelief.

Kyle tried to hold back tears and said, "He's the one that told me about you."

Dr. Gray nodded his head, "They probably found out and programmed him to do this . . . I've seen this many times before . . . Here, take this."

Dr. Gray handed Kyle Professor Hill's pistol. As they began to leave the office, Kyle spotted through a window campus police arriving.

"Quick, Dr. Gray, let's go this way!"

He followed Kyle's lead out a side door entrance as six young college-aged police entered the building with weapons drawn. Kyle and Dr. Gray quickly disappeared down into a nearby storm drain manhole.

After climbing down a ladder, they waded through a couple feet of water inside the red-lighted tunnel. Dr. Gray inquired, "Where's this go?"

Kyle pointed down the seemingly endless tunnel and said, "I really don't know. But that direction should cross under the campus."

"Fine, lead the way."

Kyle and Dr. Gray followed the red-lighted tunnel wall for some distance. They located another ladder, and Kyle climbed up. He slowly raised the manhole cover enough and got his bearings. "We're across the street from the college's main administration building," he whispered.

Kyle looked at his watch that read 10:30 p.m. "The coast is clear," he called below, and Dr. Gray began to climb the ladder. Once topside, they hid in bushes just as a stretched white limo pulled up in front of the administration building. Dr. Cummings got out of the limo and quickly entered through the front entrance door.

"Well, I'll be. My theory was right," exclaimed Dr. Gray.

"That bastard's eyes and ears seem to be everywhere at all times."

"Kyle, he always seems to know what happening here for the last twenty-five years. Come on. Let's see who he's calling on at this late hour."

Around 11:00 p.m. that Thursday night, Kyle and Dr. Gray entered Dean Witherspoon's third-floor office with their handguns drawn. Dr. Cummings and Dean Witherspoon were seated at a rectangular conference table. Student files and other documents were spread out on the table. Dr. Gray stepped into the light from the door's shadow.

"Well, well. What have we here? A little after-hours social club?"

"My, my, Dr. William Gray! Aren't you a sight for sore eyes. Right, Dean?"

"Careful, Doctor, he's got a weapon."

"It's been a while since I've seen the likes of you two," replied Dr. Gray who then said, "Dr. Cummings, Tom Witherspoon, I believe you already know my partner."

"Yes. We've all been very interested in the young Sheridan lad ever since he began his graduate studies here at Farnsworth earlier this month. I see you've paid no heed to my warnings, young man."

"That's right, Dr. Cummings, especially, when my fiancée and grandparents are being held hostages by your goons."

"Doctor! Why didn't I know anything about this hostage situation?"

"Shut up, Dean. They're my business, not yours."

"You're wrong, Doctor. Anything that involves my students is my business."

Dr. Gray ordered, "Dr. Cummings, come with us."

Just then, four campus police arrived, and a gunfight ensued. Dr. Gray and Kyle were quickly overpowered. They reluctantly were forced to surrender their weapons to the heavily armed police force.

The doctor then shouted, "No! You'll come with me now."

Kyle struggled to his feet as he was being held. He yelled back at the doctor, "You harm us and you'll never see any of your fucking money."

He quickly approached and slapped Kyle across the face. "That money was extorted from me by Henry Prestol and your father."

"You leave my daddy out of this. Today, it's between you and me."

"My, aren't we brave tonight, young Mr. Sheridan? Take them away! Dean, have my limo brought around front."

"Of course, Dr. Cummings, anything you need."

Kyle and Bill Gray were taken hostage. They had their hands bound behind them and duct tape wrapped over their mouths and eyes. They felt themselves being pushed into the backseat of another car as the rain began to fall again. From inside, they hear the doctor say good night to Dean Witherspoon.

32

Silopanna Research Center
Midnight

A black sedan with black windows pulled up in front of the building. All four campus security guards pulled Kyle and Dr. Gray out of the car. The prisoners were still bound, blindfolded, and gagged. They remained standing as Dr. Cummings's limo arrived and parked.

The doctor ordered, "Guards, put our guests with the others.

Meet me back in the lab for further instructions in fifteen minutes."

The four guards saluted and pushed Kyle and Dr. Gray inside. They were moved down a long corridor. At the end, a guard opened a solid-metal fire door. Ten jail cells lined each wall. One cell housed Jen and another, Kyle's grandparents, Richard, Sr., and Mary Sheridan.

Jen approached the cell bars and saw Kyle. She called out, "Kyle! Are you hurt?"

Grandpa remained seated in the cell and told her, "He's not hurt, just his damn ego."

Grandma stood up and began weeping. She called out to Kyle, "You just couldn't leave the past alone. How could you get us into this horrible place?"

Jen then whispered to Grandpa, "Who's the other man?"

"That's the shrink, Bill Gray. He's one that belongs in here."

Kyle and Dr. Gray were paraded past then and pushed into separate cells. Each man fell to the floor and squirmed helplessly in their restraints.

Meanwhile, in the research center's medical lab, Dr. Cummings prepared injections for his new guests. He said to himself, "This combination of LSD and Sernyl should soften all their little minds. The right dosage may cause enough side effects to permanently disable them all."

He then yelled, "Guards! Bring me the prisoners!"

Shortly, all five of the prisoners were escorted under armed guards into the lab and were strapped to restraining devices. Jen was strapped separately to a hospital gurney. The tape was then removed from Kyle's and Dr. Gray's eyes. They stared in horror at the sight.

During this same time period, Special Forces commandos, under special instructions from the U.S. Attorney General's Office, overpowered the youthful campus police and silently entered the warehouse. They placed explosive charges near the base of the east wall of the research lab and moved back into seclusion to await further instructions.

Dr. Cummings approached his prisoners in their restraints. He took off Kyle's gag. Kyle spat at him.

"My, my, such manners. Didn't your grandparents here teach you manners?"

"Yes. They taught me to hate bastards like you!"

"Never mind, Kyle. Your time is up. I don't see a bag containing the money from my ransom demands."

"You idiot! The money is not in some fucking bank, you asshole!"

The old medical doctor shouted back, "And I still expected you to get it!"

"I don't believe there is any money."

"But because you have disappointed me, I'll send Ms. Howser on a nice trip once she's injected."

Kyle helplessly yelled, "You pervert! Leave my fiancée alone!"

The doctor held a hypodermic needle close to the wide-eyed and gagged Jen and said, "Oh, she'll be alone someday . . . in a sanitarium. She'll be going insane from this overdose . . . just like all you others. Watch . . ."

Suddenly, the building's lights went out as an explosion occurred outside the lab and a section of the wall caved in, creating a hole. Heavily armed U.S. Special Forces, wearing night vision visors immediately began to enter through the wall opening.

The doctor, who was momentarily stunned, turned from Jen and yelled, "Guards! Protect my prisoners! Kill all those damn meddling commandos!"

The lights flickered as the commandos immediately opened fire and killed several guards. Dr. Gray was shot by Dr. Cummings. Kyle managed to break free and jumped on top of the doctor. In the scuffle, Kyle got Cummings's pistol and shots him, killing him instantly.

Kyle jumps off the doctor and frees Jen. Other commandos release Richard and Mary and take the remainder of Cummings's men prisoners. Dr. Gray lay mortally wounded. He slowly motioned for Jen to come closer to him. She hastened to his side.

Whispering, he tells her, "Jennifer, I must confess something."

Jen held his head up. "Please don't try to talk, Dr. Gray. The medics will be here soon."

He began to cough. Recovering enough to speak, he said in a weak voice, "I'm your real father."

Startled at what she thought she heard, she asked, "What did you say?"

"I made love to Melanie Dulane when she was drugged in Fort Douglas's lab back in July 1971. She never knew it. When she found out she was pregnant and eventually gave birth to her daughter, Jennifer, in April 1972, Dr. Cummings programmed Ricky Sheridan to claim responsibility."

Kyle approached and knelt down. "So my late uncle Ricky was not Jen's father."

"No, I was. Kyle, show her the love I never could . . ."

Dr. Gray died on the lab floor cradled by a weeping Jen with Kyle kneeling along his side. Kyle's grandparents stepped forward. Richard put his hand on Kyle's shoulder and softly said, "Your grandmother and I are very sorry about the other day and our jumping to wrong conclusions."

Kyle stood up with tears in his eyes. "My life with Jen will have no more lies. Both her and my parents seemed to be victims of that perverted old army doctor lying over there."

"Yes, Kyle. He hurt many people. Now it's your duty to set the records and files straight," commented Mary.

Both Kyle and Jen affirmed, "We will. We promise."

33

Day Twelve
Fort Douglas
Main Gate
Early Morning

Kyle, Jen, along with his grandparents, Richard, Sr., and Mary were escorted off base as Special Forces commandos continued to round up Cummings's henchmen.

"Look at all those poor students who were programmed by the doctor," said Kyle.

Jen added, "Well, at least now they'll get proper treatment and probably enter a true rehab program."

Kyle and Jennifer, once again reunited from their harrowing ordeal, simply melted into each other's arms. His grandparents were, once again safe and sound, at home. They finally knew the real truth about their late sons' involvement in the scheme of treachery and deception that the army so secretly concealed and denied.

Jen and Kyle felt so relieved that they were not blood related. But Jen was terribly saddened to now know that Dr. Gray was her biological father.

"Why did he hide from me all those years?" she cried.

"I suppose even if he actually knew who adopted you at eleven months, he had to have been sworn to secrecy about the project," commented Kyle. "Besides, if word would have leaked out about him having sex with his pretty young female lab volunteers, his ass surely would have been grass!"

Kyle looked with compassion at the beautiful mother-to-be and held her close. Jen simply cried for such a long time while clinging to his strong shoulders.

Around noon, dressed like they were a team of archeologists armed with gloves, a bag of hand tools, and a flashlight, Kyle and Jennifer stood once again at the front entrance to the old abandoned stone farmhouse. In his hands were the two folded Mercantile pieces of paper from their discovery Saturday, a week ago. They had been recovered from the metal box beneath the attic floorboards. Kyle unfolded the papers and commented, "The one rectangle does resemble the shape of this structure. It appears not to be in scale though."

Pointing toward an opening in the bottom line, Jen said, "If this line break denotes the front door location, the other structure would be over in that direction."

They both walked around the left side of the old house and saw no evidence of another building.

"Come on, follow me."

The ground was covered with knee-high tall thorny briers. The young couple stepped cautiously. Jen cried out several times as the thorns stuck her.

After they had traversed a couple hundred yards from the old house, Kyle noticed several piles of stacked stones well overgrown with vegetation. "These stones could be part of the barn's foundation."

After using his garden-gloved hands to pull the weeds and undergrowth away, a section of cut stones emerged. "This could well be the barn's foundation corner," he told her.

"Look down there," she said, pointing. "That's a concrete floor!"

"I see that now. Hand me the other piece of paper."

Eyeing the sketch, he saw the smaller rectangle in the upper corner of the larger one. "Come on, follow me."

After struggling to cover about fifty feet more, they began climbing over several large hand-honed wooden beams that appeared to be charcoal burnt.

"These definitely were used in post and beam barn construction in the eighteenth Century."

"Great, now where do we look?" Jen said, feeling slightly overwhelmed from the hike.

"Wait here, darling. You need to sit and take it easy. I'll scout around and call you if I find anything."

"Please be careful. This time of year brings out the critters."

Kyle soon realized he was walking on a vine-covered concrete floor. Near the edge of the pad, he noticed an exposed section that was reinforced with steel rebars and about eight inches thick. "Why so thick a fucking floor? Commercial garages only have six inches of concrete," he pondered. "This could hold tons of weight, like military type vehicles."

He was not out of Jen's sight when he located something strange. The concrete floor had abruptly stopped, and he was standing on a metal panel. Reaching down, he tried to lift up an edge. Taking his hammer to it, he succeeded in chipping off a small piece. Kneeling down, he aimed his flashlight down into the dark space below.

"Jen, I've found something like a cellar under this part of the slab."

Peering into the space, he could see a faded yellow "Civil Defense" sign indicating an underground fallout shelter entrance.

"There's a fucking bomb shelter down there!" he exclaimed. "It must be something from the Cold War era of the 1950s."

"Interesting," she commented. "Nikita Khrushchev would have been proud of your discovery."

"Who?" he called back from inside the shelter.

"He was the premier of the former Soviet Union during the 1962 Cuban Missile Crisis. He and our President, John F. Kennedy, had both countries very close to a nuclear war. Lots of fearful citizens had fallout shelters built to withstand an atomic blast."

Walking back to her, he said, "That's my history buff Jen."

"You should read history sometimes. You'll learn stuff!" She laughed.

"It makes sense now with Fort Douglas being so close. The Russians might have had it as a prime target."

Together they approached the hatch cover. "I want to check this baby out."

"Oh, I don't know if it's safe to explore. It's pretty old and could possibly be unstable."

"I'm not an atomic blast." He frowned. "Just gotta hunch, that's all."

"And what's that, darling?"

"Ah, I don't know. Just another unusual place to have sex?" he smiled.

"Behave! Go ahead and look. I'll stand guard."

With the help of an old piece of timber as a shim, Kyle used his brute strength and managed to slide the heavy armored hatch open enough to slide inside. Jen handed him the toolbox and his flashlight.

Evening was approaching, and she was becoming anxious again. Within a short while, Kyle's head emerged and she helped him climb back up. She was delighted to see him but concerned for his exploration report.

"It's pretty creepy down there. The walls are concrete and lined with wooden shelves full of nonperishable food items, along with sleeping bunks and an electric generator."

"Yes, please tell me if you found anything else."

"Oh yes, there was something else," he said with a broad grin.

"What else did you find?"

"A huge fucking safe! With the word Mercantile stenciled on the door."

"What! A safe?! For real!" she exclaimed.

"The other sheet of Mercantile Bank paper had the combination to that safe on it."

"You actually opened it!"

"Yep. It appears that old Professor Henry Prestol, aka Ms. Trisha Alexander, must have converted all the money from Dr. Cummings's research grants, the money from Uncle Ricky's and my daddy's drug selling, along with the cash wired from Henry's brother, David, in Vietnam, into gold bars stashed inside that huge old safe!"

"Oh my god! Kyle, is it possible that you have located what all those people wanted enough to kill for but could never find?"

"They spent their lives wanting just a piece of the pie, and Henry controlled everything. And each went to their graves over that money."

34

Over the next several days, professionals from the Mercantile Bank assisted Kyle and Jennifer in moving the gold bars from the underground vault. The gold was carefully loaded, under armed guards, into an armored truck and escorted to the bank in Harrisburg. At the current rate of exchange, gold in October 1994 was hovering around four hundred dollars an ounce! Kyle's treasure weighed in close to thirty million dollars.

Several trust funds were then established, along with scholarships for gifted but underprivileged students to attend Farnsworth College. People from all walks of life became entangled in that web of destruction and greed between 1968 and 1976. Those included hundreds of innocent college students merely seeking to connect to an easily accessible free drug scene. The participants included brilliant facility educators, administrators, and many top military and medical professionals. Not to be forgotten were the families torn apart by senseless violence and jealousy. And least but most important were the children of this generation who were spawned from communal living, multiple sex partners, orgies, drugs, and booze.

Kyle and Jennifer, along with their love for each other and their new baby, John Paul Sheridan, Jr., can now finally again find happiness as a family.

Epilogue

The springtime campus was readied for the noontime dedication ceremony. Flowering dogwood trees and azaleas surrounded the quad. Media and invited guests were assembled.

Dean Thomas Witherspoon presided and said, "Good day, everyone. Please be seated. A Farnsworth welcome is extended to members of our faculty, students, parents, and invited guests. Today we are truly pleased that two members of this year's graduating class have chosen to present this special memorial plaque. In addition, today they have brought along a most generous gift to the endowment fund. I would like to present Mr. and Mrs. Kyle Sheridan and their infant son, John Paul Sheridan, Jr."

Everyone present stood and applauded as the young couple with their baby moved to the podium.

Kyle addressed the group saying, "Thank you, Dean. Everyone, please be seated. Today we have come to honor the memory of certain very gifted young people whose lives were cut short, not in war nor by illness, but by simple greed of a few misguided individuals. They regretfully met and used this beloved institution as a base for a covert and perverted operation. Those of us who knew these persons are now forever changed. What my lovely wife, the former Jennifer Howser, and

I discovered last September opened our eyes to an unbelievable chain of events that had its origins here more that twenty-five years ago."

Jen moved to the mike after placing the tiny sleeping infant in Kyle's strong arms. She said, "The names on this plaque belong to students and faculty members who died from a secret pact, made between our college community and the U.S. Army medical research program at Fort Douglas in January 1969. What some people did was very wrong. They could not function normally following their participation in the research program. Many of these individuals were given overdoses and, sadly, committed suicide. Evidence now rediscovered showed that both of my husband parents, John and Suzanne Sheridan, John's brother, Richard Sheridan, Jr., and my own parents, Melanie Dulane and former psychology professor Dr. William Gray, were research participants and eventually became its victims. Dean Witherspoon, if you would."

The dean unveiled the wall plaque while the invited guests applauded.

Jen continued, "This plaque also includes the names of the late dean, Dr. Joseph Henson, chemistry professor Henry Prestol, political science professor Roger Hill, and forty other Farnsworth students from 1969 through 1976."

As each name of a victim was read, a bell tolled from the college's chapel bell tower. Once completed, Kyle and Jen turned to Dean Witherspoon who graciously accepted a check for ten million dollars.

Together, all four were photographed in front of the commemorative plaque.

THE END